A Boy From
Bethesda

A Boy From
Bethesda

Dennis McKay

iUniverse LLC
Bloomington

A Boy From Bethesda

iUniverse books may be ordered through booksellers or by contacting:

iUniverse LLC
1663 Liberty Drive
Bloomington, IN 47403
www.iuniverse.com
1-800-Authors (1-800-288-4677)

ISBN: 978-1-4759-8591-7 (sc)
ISBN: 978-1-4759-8592-4 (e)

Printed in the United States of America

iUniverse rev. date: 04/28/2014

CONTENTS

Chapter 1

Ayrlawn

Go gently into the night, Johnny, me boy, go gently . . .

It was Bethesda back in the day. The early summer air was mild, but a southerly breeze hinted at a change around the corner. A boy wearing a gray T-shirt, khaki shorts, and black Keds was walking with purposeful strides down Hempstead Street, his trusty mitt a visor from the afternoon sun. He paid little mind to the Cape Cods, red-brick colonials, and split levels with tidy yards and glistening green foliage as he took everything in with that quick, keen-eyed look of youthful anticipation. The year was 1956, and at that moment, all things seemed possible to ten-year-old Johnny O'Brien, a good-looking, dark-haired lad with a finely cut face with a pinch of pink in the cheeks.

A 1948 four-door Packard that was parked in a driveway diverted his attention, its bulky, black exterior all shiny and sparkly in the sunlight. He veered over to the car and peeked inside the open front window, admiring the spacious backseat and tan interior. When he was younger, Johnny could name nearly every car on the road by the design of the rear bumper and tail fin, but he couldn't any longer. His interests had changed.

After a few blocks, Hempstead Street ended at a rather long and new-looking school with a bright brick façade, probably a junior high by its size, but it was not what Johnny was looking for. He removed a baseball from the web of his mitt, flicking it into the pocket in a repetitive motion as he looked to his left and right down the intersecting street—nothing but more homes. He decided to turn around.

Around the corner from the house he and his parents had moved into earlier in the day, Johnny came upon a wooden placard supported by two posts with Ayrlawn Recreation Center carved into the face. At the bottom of a little hill was the rec center that his mother had told him was somewhere nearby. Ayrlawn was a long and wide expanse of grass, nearly big enough to hold two full-sized football fields. In a corner off to his left, there was a backstop and at the far end another even larger backstop. Across the field, an asphalt basketball court snagged his attention, and on a raised area next to the basketball court was a barn with a silo shaped like a rocket ship looming over it. Atop the silo was a faded green weathervane in the shape of a cow. "Wow," Johnny said under his breath. "Wow."

He scooted down the hill to the nearest backstop that had a Little-League-size dirt infield, its left field merging into the right field of the other backstop. The second backstop had a major-league-size infield with a pitcher's mound with a rubber, no less. Left field ended at two tennis courts enclosed by a high chain-link fence, and next to it Johnny came to the basketball court, where a boy wearing a first baseman's mitt, with claw-style webbing, was throwing a tennis ball against a brick wall.

This kid had the look of a ballplayer, with wide shoulders anchoring a well-proportioned body, his coordinated overhand throwing motion effortless as only a left-hander could do.

"Hey, Lefty," Johnny said, waving his baseball. "Wanna play catch?"

"Sure." The boy trotted over, and they tossed the ball back and forth. "You new here?"

"Moved in today." Johnny held the ball for a moment, stealing another look around, still not believing this treasure trove of Ayrlawn. "Did this used to be a farm?"

"Yeah," the left-hander said, catching the ball. "Really neat, huh?" He inspected the baseball, which had barely a scratch on it. "New ball?"

"Pretty much," Johnny said. "What's your name?"

"Danny, Danny McKenzie." He raised his chin as if to say, *What's yours?*

"Johnny O'Brien." Johnny tossed the ball to Danny. "Give me some grounders." Danny leaned his head in the direction of the big backstop. "Let's go over there, and I'll throw them to you from first base." Danny squinted at Johnny. "Shortstop, right?"

"Uh huh," Johnny said as they began to walk over, "but my favorite player is Mickey Mantle."

"Me and another kid took the streetcar from Bethesda down to Griffith Stadium and saw him play."

"I've been there too, but the Senators played Kansas City," Johnny said with a little shake of the head. "But I did get Vic Power's autograph."

Danny trotted over to where first base would be and drew the outline of the base with a stick. He threw Johnny a slow roller that he charged, scooped up barehanded, and threw off balance underhand. Danny extended his right leg nearly into a split, stretched his glove out, and caught the ball before it could hit the ground.

"Nice stretch," Johnny said with a nod.

"Way to hustle," Danny said, pointing his glove at Johnny. They were two ballplayers perfectly at ease in this timeless ritual, a feeling-out period when each boy was fielding his position and at the same time checking out the other.

After a while, Danny's friends appeared, and they organized a game. Some of the boys were wary of Johnny, this new kid who was obviously such a good ballplayer. It wasn't in what they said but what they didn't say, never speaking directly to Johnny, as though they were members of a private club. But on the new kid's first day, Danny made it clear that Johnny was his friend—picking him first, batting him third, and playing him at shortstop. By the end of the week, it was understood that Johnny O'Brien was the best ballplayer at Ayrlawn and one of them, a boy from Bethesda.

*   *   *

On a Saturday morning in the autumn of Johnny's first year at Ayrlawn, he arrived early to get the place all to himself before his friends showed up, a little ritual of his. It was one of those crystal-clear October days with nary a cloud in the sky. Ribbons of light stretched across the trees, their flickering leaves showing the first blushes of gold and red. There was a chill in the air but with a promise of warmth. All of it made Johnny feel as if he belonged to something special.

He stood at the edge of the asphalt basketball court, slinging his baseball—now scuffed and grass-stained after a summer of abuse—against the brick wall that was separated from the court by a weedy strip of dirt. When the ball hit a rock and took a bad hop, Johnny's lean body sprang up from a crouched position, his elbows drawn back and the mitt raised upward to secure the ball without missing a beat. His throwing motion was fluid and quick, as were his reflexes when scooping the ball into his mitt and returning it to the wall. From the corner of his eye, he saw Danny approaching the basketball court. "Where are the rest of the guys?"

"They're coming, Johnny," Danny said as he jerked his thumb back over his shoulder toward a gaggle of boys emerging from a line of trees at the corner of the field behind the little backstop. Their garbled, yapping voices—happy noise to Johnny's ears—carried across the field, with Mickey, Yogi, and the Duke registering above the fray in reverent bursts.

"They're still excited about the Series," Danny said as they headed toward the big backstop.

"It was really something to get to listen to in it class," Johnny said. One of the boys had sneaked a transistor radio into the classroom for game seven of the World Series between the New York Yankees and Brooklyn Dodgers. "In my old school, the nuns would never have allowed a radio in the classroom."

"I heard they're really strict," Danny said as he waved the other boys over to the big backstop.

"Mean, too," Johnny said with meaning as he hurled the ball high in the air and ran forward to catch it. He turned back to Danny and said, "Nothing scarier than hearing their gowns swishing and the rosary beads clickety-clacking when they're storming down the hallway."

"Yeah," Danny said, more as a question.

"It means some kid is about to get grabbed by the collar and smacked hard across the face."

Danny stopped in his tracks and turned to Johnny. "Really?" He started to walk again and said, "They ever hit you?"

They were on the edge of the dirt infield between second and third. "No," Johnny said as he spun the ball backwards out of his hand, catching it over and over. "I never gave them anything to get mad about." He snatched the ball out of the air and cocked it behind his ear as if to throw it to first. "Some of the boys never seemed to learn, though."

A few more kids showed up, and soon they had six on a side: a pitcher, three infielders, and two outfielders. The game started with Mickey Doyle pitching to Tip Durham. On the first pitch, Tip smashed a one-hopper to short that rocketed off the hard-baked infield surface. Johnny glided to his left, crossed his mitt over his body, caught the ball on the rise, and threw off his back foot to first, beating the runner by a step.

Next batter up was Tip's cousin, who was visiting from New York. He was a year older than the rest of the boys and had that swagger about him like one of the Bowery Boys. On his first pitch, Mickey slipped, and the ball whizzed toward the cousin's head, causing him to duck and fall away from home plate, landing him on his fanny. He sprang up and dusted the dirt off the rear of his jeans—the other boys all wore shorts—and squinted at Mickey. "Hey, Howdy Doody, what kinda rag-arm shit is dat?"

"Shut up and hit," Mickey said, blushing bright red. He didn't really look like Howdy Doody. His face was leaner and well formed. But Mickey did have reddish-brown hair and patches of freckles on his face—a wear-your-heart-on-your-sleeve kinda face—enough, it seemed, for Tip's cousin to make fun of.

Back and forth it went as the game came to a standstill while pitcher and batter traded barbs. "Get somebody in here dat can pitch?"

"*Dat?*" Mickey said in a mocking voice. "Can't you say *that?*" The cousin, who was built like a tugboat—thick-necked and stout, a tough-looking kid—stomped toward Mickey with bat in hand, his lips drawn tight, his dark eyes two smoldering embers in the glare of the sun.

As the taller, lankier Mickey stood his ground, Johnny bolted in from shortstop and blocked the boy's path. "Hold on," Johnny said, raising his hand like a traffic cop.

"Git out of the way." The cousin tried to step around, but Johnny moved in front of him. Whichever way the cousin went, Johnny blocked his path, gliding from side to side, quick on his feet. Finally the boy lunged at Johnny, who sprang back. The boy fell flat on his face, the bat landing at Johnny's feet.

"Yah-hah," Mickey taunted the boy, who was spitting dirt and dust out of his mouth.

"Enough, Mickey." Johnny bent down and offered his hand. The boy scrambled to his feet on his own and faced Johnny. "Ya wanna fight?"

Tip, who was smaller than the other boys, rushed in and grabbed his cousin's arm. "Come on, Lenny."

Lenny jerked away from Tip and turned his attention back to Johnny, fist clenched and cocked. "I said, you wanna fight?"

"I'd rather play baseball," Johnny said as he handed the boy the bat. "You're up."

Lenny looked at the bat and then at Johnny, not sure what his next move should be.

Johnny flashed an easy smile. "Tip told us you saw Mickey Mantle hit that homer off Ramos at Yankee Stadium that almost left the park."

"Yeah, what about it?"

"That must have been exciting."

"You like the Mick?"

"We all love the Mick," Johnny said.

"Yeah," Lenny said, unclenching his fist. "Okay, then."

He returned to the batter's box. Mickey's next pitch was a strike, and Lenny swung with all he had. He didn't get all of it and hit a blooper to short left field. Johnny raced back, his head turned as he followed the flight of the ball. With arms extended, he caught the ball on a dead run.

"Great play," Mickey shouted, pumping his fist at Johnny. "That was a big-league play."

Over the course of the game, Johnny stretched all out for a grounder to his left, stepped on second to get the lead runner, and fired a bullet to Danny at first base for a double play. And to top it off, he won the game by blasting a drive to left field that didn't stop until it trickled up to the fence of the empty tennis court—home run.

They played until noon with no more fireworks between Mickey and Lenny. By then they were all thirsty and hungry. The boys collected their bats, balls, and mitts and trudged on toward home, agreeing to meet back in an hour for another game. At the top of the little hill, Johnny waved so long and told them not to be late for the next game.

Lenny came over to Johnny and stuck out his hand, which Johnny shook. "I'm heading home soon, but wanna tell ya that you're a helluva of ballplayer," Lenny said.

"Thanks," Johnny said through a grin. "Say hi for me to the Mick next time you see him."

Lenny cocked his head appraisingly at Johnny. "You're all right." He nodded as though to confirm his words. "Yeah, you're all right."

Johnny headed for his house around the corner, a Cape Cod situated on a rise behind Ayrlawn. He and his parents had previously lived in an apartment in northwest DC with nowhere nearby to play ball. The place had been a somber-looking ten-story structure, the tenants mostly older people. It even had that old-person smell in the hallways that reminded Johnny of the funeral home for his grandfather's funeral. He had made only one friend in the building, Buzzy Morgan, a boy two years older who had no interest in sports but loved cars. Buzzy had picked up this trait from his father, who would take Johnny and Buzzy for rides on Sunday afternoons, pointing out the name and year of every car they passed.

But by age eight, Johnny's interest in cars had waned as it seemed his growing body craved to throw, catch, and shoot balls—any kind of ball would do. He began to take the streetcar down to the Jelleff Boys Club in Georgetown, where there was a ball field and gym. But often the gym wasn't open, or there weren't enough kids at the ball field to play a game. Two boys were usually there, though, brothers Chris and John Dillon, a couple of big athletic kids from Johnny's grade school, who were regulars. Often, the three would play catch and throw batting practice to each other while the third boy shagged. So to be able to come home from school and have Ayrlawn right next door had opened up an entirely new world for Johnny, a joyous world where he felt free and no longer trapped in that dank, old apartment that was always too hot in the winter and even worse in the summertime.

His parents had wanted him to continue in Catholic school, but after making friends at Ayrlawn who were all in public school, they relented. So he no longer had to wear a uniform to school or cringe at the swishing of an angry nun's habit.

At Wyngate Elementary School, Johnny's fifth grade teacher was a first for him—a man. Mr. Grayson was tall and baldhead and wore thick-framed glasses that he was constantly pushing back up the bridge of his nose. He was a no-nonsense disciplinarian, but he never put a hand on any of the boys when they acted up. A kid might wing a spitball across the room while Mr. Grayson's back was to the class. The teacher would turn and walk right over to the guilty party and lean his head toward a stool in a corner in the front of the class. "Take a seat, Mr. Doyle." None of the boys knew how he did it. Mickey said he must have had some sort of superpower.

It was all so different. Instead of walking by himself on city streets to school, dressed in his blue blazer and tie amongst the bustle of honking horns and the jangled clang of streetcars rattling down the middle of the street, Johnny now cut through the woods with Danny and meandered through the Ayrlawn and Wyngate neighborhoods to get to and from school. And he could actually wear his Keds to school.

Not that Johnny had been unhappy before. He didn't realize it, but his new home and school were a big improvement on his old life. His new house wasn't as nice as some of his friends' homes, many of which were bigger with modern kitchens, but his little white box of a home nestled under a weeping willow suited him just fine.

More than fine, Johnny thought. He was surprised to see his father's '52 Chevy sedan still in the driveway. "A smooth-looking hunk of US steel," his father had chirped to Johnny the day he

9

had purchased the car, a rare moment of cheer from his usual dour demeanor.

Johnny opened the front door of his house into a small foyer that opened to the living room/dining room space, which was separated only by the variation in furnishings. The floor was covered by beige wall-to-wall carpeting that his mother had insisted on before they moved in. "My one and only extravagance that I ask for, Ed," she had told her husband.

Mary O'Brien was in the kitchen, wearing her smock apron with tiny red polka dots over her white buttoned-down blouse and gray skirt. She had a filter-tipped cigarette between her ring and middle finger, while in the other hand a wooden spatula stirred a pot of stew on the stove, the warm, comfortable smell lingering in the air.

Johnny's mother looked over her shoulder and smiled, parting her lips, which were coated by bright-red lipstick to reveal a row of sparkling white teeth. "Hello, honey." She was a fine-looking, full-figured woman with wavy, raven-black hair cut above the shoulder in a soft tumble of curls, her eyes dark blue and lovely and her skin white like ivory. Mary's sister had told Johnny he was a thinner, male version of his mother. "You are as Black Irish handsome as she is pretty."

"Isn't Dad bowling today?" His father's lone passion was a Saturday bowling league at an alley in downtown Bethesda.

"Wasn't feeling well, honey," his mother replied. "He thinks he's coming down with something." She smiled again and tilted her head to the side, her eyes crinkling up at the edges. It was a look Johnny had come to know, a look that said, *Not to worry.* "He's resting in our bedroom." She took a long drag on her cigarette and blew a stream of smoke out the side of her mouth. "Now, what would you like for lunch?" She flicked an ash from her cigarette into an ashtray on the windowsill. "I bought you a treat—Ovaltine."

While Johnny was eating at the dining room table, he heard a bedroom door off the hallway creak open and the heavy thud of his father's footsteps. Ed O'Brien appeared in his stocking feet—black socks were all he ever wore—wearing trousers and a sleeveless T-shirt. He was a stocky, balding man with a perpetual five o'clock shadow, a regular-looking dad save the constant, unsmiling look of someone trying to get through each day without complications or aggravation.

Johnny felt a little uncomfortable around his father, never sure what to say. They exchanged glances, and then his father dropped his gaze to Johnny's half-eaten peanut butter and jelly on rye. He looked back up at his son and nodded hello, his eyes half-sleepy, half-grumpy, the color drained from his face. He looked into the cramped, rectangular-shaped kitchen through the doorless doorway where his wife was trying to eliminate the crackly static on the clock radio sitting on the windowsill, unaware of his presence. She enjoyed listening to her gardening show every Saturday while dutifully sponging the speckled-green Formica countertop, mopping the already clean linoleum floor, or preparing a meal. She could stand at her sink, piddling away for hours, gazing occasionally out the window with a view of Hempstead Avenue, her street, in her very own house.

"Mary," Ed said, leaning his head into the kitchen.

She turned from the sink and wiped her hands on her apron, a thin, neutral smile on her lips. "Feeling better, Ed?"

"No," he said as he stole a glance at Johnny, who was sitting there as if waiting for something to happen. Ed lifted his chin toward his son. "Go ahead, eat." His tone wasn't mean but sort of indifferent. Johnny took a bite of his sandwich and then washed it down with a swig of milk. His father pursed his lips, nodded ever so slightly, and then turned his attention back to the kitchen. "Mary, where is the aspirin?"

She took a quick drag on her cigarette, put it out in the ashtray, and turned off the radio. "It's where it always is, Ed," she said as she came into the dining room, "in the medicine cabinet."

He looked at her, his eyes saying, *Will you find it for me?*

"I'll get it," said Mary.

Johnny felt even more uncomfortable and self-conscious with his mother out of the room. He kept his eyes down and worked on finishing his sandwich, even though his appetite had suddenly disappeared.

His mother returned and handed her husband two aspirin. "Would you also like me to pour you a glass of water, Ed?" Her tone indicated a trace of aggravation that he had ruined her happy moment.

"Yes, as a matter of fact," Ed said, "I would."

Mary returned with a glass of water and handed it to her husband. Ed swallowed the tablets, handed the water back to his wife, stood there for an unsure moment, and then turned from the room and went back down the hallway. The click of the bedroom door shutting sent a wave of relief over Johnny—not that he was afraid of his dad, but more that he wasn't comfortable around him and always a little nervous when his parents had their little encounters, as if they might take it up a notch into one of their arguments. They were short-lived events with bursts of shouting and finger-pointing before his father stormed off, mumbling under his breath.

Like a lot of men from his generation, Ed O'Brien was not a touchy-feely sort of father. He never played catch with his son or spent time with him other than at the dinner table. He was a cartographer for the Army Corps of Engineers, a trade he had learned in the military during WWII. He was a reliable, steady man, an even-keel sort of guy who came home from work every evening, had a cocktail with his wife before dinner, and afterwards read the evening paper. Every Saturday, he bowled in his league and then came home and took a nap, a man of routine. He wasn't abusive or cruel to his son; he just didn't pay him much attention.

Immediately after his father left the room, Johnny's appetite returned, and his mother went into the kitchen and made him another sandwich. When she put the plate in front of her son, she offered a half smile, half grimace, which caused the corners of her mouth to droop, a look Johnny was familiar with and that he interpreted as an apology for his father's indifference.

After lunch, Johnny headed on back to Ayrlawn. A fleeting thought of the rarity of his dad staying home from bowling due to his not feeling well flew from his mind as the ball field came into view.

Johnny was early. He sat under a stand of trees on a rise near the big backstop and waited. He imagined he was sitting in an end zone section of Ayrlawn, and the green cow weather vane, or Moo Moo, as the boys called it, was like a unique team mascot whirling away high overhead at the other end of the field. He pounded his fist into his mitt, a Rawlings Mickey Mantle model that he had gotten for his tenth birthday last April. It had been the biggest thrill of his life. Even his father seemed to realize the impact on his son when he said with a trace of enthusiasm, "I got you a glove same as the one your hero wears." Johnny had oiled the mitt and then put a baseball in the pocket and tied a string around it for three days to break it in. But then he had hardly used it until they moved to Bethesda, where almost every day this past summer, he had played baseball at Ayrlawn. He brought the pocket of his mitt to his face, smelling the scent of leather and oil. Oh, yeah, how great it smelled, and how great it was to get to play ball every day.

When all the kids showed up, they chose new teams and played for three more hours until, by late afternoon, they were all spent. But what a day it had been—baseball in the morning and afternoon, a doubleheader.

Heading home, Johnny felt happy-tired, a kind of joy that today had been, maybe, the best day ever. When his house came into view, he saw a long, white vehicle parked behind his dad's car in the driveway. He squinted to make out what it was, maybe a Cadillac.

As he neared, Johnny made out Bethesda Chevy Chase Rescue Squad stenciled in black on the side of the back door. He raced home, his legs churning, arms pumping. As he reached for the front door, it swung open. Johnny jumped back, startled, as two men in crisp white shirts, wearing white hats with hard black brims, maneuvered a gurney over the threshold. An army-green blanket covered a body; only a pair of feet wearing black socks were exposed.

The gurney clanged onto the front stoop, and the covering slipped off to reveal his father, his face grayish-white and his head off to the side, the eyes shut and the lips parted in an uncertain crimp as though he had never seen it coming.

"Dad! Dad!" Johnny screamed as another man from the rescue squad took him gently by the arm and guided him to his mother standing at the front door, her usually pleasant face a terrified grimace.

"Come inside, honey," she said in a voice drained of emotion. They sat in the living room, Johnny on the sofa under the bay window and his mother in a high-arched chair facing her only child. "Your father most likely had a heart attack, Johnny." She folded her hands as though praying and rested them under her chin. "He's dead. Your father is dead."

"What?" Johnny said in a trembling voice as he felt a swell of panic swarm in his throat. His world of happy-tired replaced by confusion and fear.

His mother came over next to him, wrapped her arm around his shoulder, and brought him into her side. "I'm so sorry, honey, so sorry." Johnny felt disoriented, as though this home that he adored seemed so different, so small and cold and unwelcoming with death in the air.

One of the men from the rescue squad stood slump-shouldered in the foyer, a strained expression on his face. He leaned his head forward and tipped his fingers to the brim of his hat. "We'll be off now, ma'am," he said in almost a whisper.

Johnny's mother looked up at the man, her eyes those of a deer caught in the headlights. "Thank you," she said to the man. "Thank you."

The click of the door closing sent a shudder through Johnny. Then he heard the rumbly roar of the ambulance driving off until it faded away, and all that remained was the numbing silence.

Not long after, there was a tap at the front door. Johnny leaned in tight against his mother, afraid of what was coming next. Another tap, tap. Mary took a deep breath and said, "Come in."

The door opened, and a priest from Our Lady of Lourdes Church entered. He stood in the foyer for a moment as though to get his bearings. He was an older man with tired eyes, dressed in his white clerical collar and black. "Mary," he said, "I am so terribly sorry for your loss."

Mary offered her hand toward a chair. "Please, Monsignor Conley, have a seat." He sat in the high-arched chair, reached over, and patted Mary's hand. He folded his hands on his lap, looking at Mary with a mixture of priestly modesty and strain.

As the priest spoke to Johnny's mom, everything in the room appeared to be out of focus to Johnny. The walls seemed to have no corners or color, the furniture vague shapes, and the priest a blurry figure in faded black. No longer could Johnny make out the deep crevices slashed across Monsignor Conley's cheeks or the little spiny blue veins under his eyes as he continued, "I took the liberty of contacting Pumphrey's Funeral Home . . ." While the priest continued, his words audible but not heard by Johnny, the boy clung to his mother, her ample body providing a warm reassurance that he was not alone.

The remainder of the day was a blur. The priest departed, and then some neighbors arrived, but no children. Time seemed to slow down as Johnny sat, in one of the folding chairs a neighbor had brought over, in the back of the living room. Women—seeming to move in exaggerated movements like puppets being pulled by strings—set up the dining room table with bowls of casseroles and a serving plate stacked with sandwiches. One of the women began to move toward Johnny; as she neared, he saw in her eyes a look of concerned compassion. Her words seemed to float in the air, almost as if they were independent of each other. "Would . . . You . . . Like . . . A . . . Sandwich . . . Johnny?"

It took him a moment to respond as he tried to comprehend. "No thanks," he said, looking over at his mother sitting on the sofa with a neighbor woman on each side of her. She seemed so very far away, sitting there in her apron, her face a ghostly white, her eyes darting about the room until they settled on Johnny for a moment before her attention was diverted. He wanted so desperately for everyone to leave. Didn't they know that he needed his mother?

Finally, when Johnny's mother said goodbye to the last of the neighbors, the house once again fell silent. It seemed as if all the joyous life had been peeled off the walls and had left Johnny and his mother to deal with the remains. The women had cleaned up and put the leftover food in the refrigerator. The house was so very tidy and neat. Johnny's mother turned from the door and stood there for a moment, looking down. "Oh," she said in a meek voice of discovery as she untied the back sashes of her apron, slipped out from under it, and then folded it. She looked at Johnny, who hadn't left the folding chair since the first guest had arrived. "Have you eaten, honey?"

Johnny saw clearly his mother's sadness etched on her face. Mary came over to her son and kneeled down in front of him. Johnny leaned forward. She put her hands on his arms and brought him into her, burying his face in the crook of her neck. He felt the tears well in his eyes, his first tears.

That night, lying in his bed, Johnny could hear his mother sobbing. He had never heard her cry, or for that matter any adult cry. He was already scared, and her cries sent a hollow chill through him. The sobs came in ear-cracking waves of anguish. Then there was momentary silence before it started again. Johnny rolled over on his side, cupping his hand over his ear, trying to pretend none of this was happening.

Finally, he turned on the light on his nightstand. He went down the hallway and stood at her door. The sobs now were like low murmurs, as if she had cried herself out. "Mom," he said in a brave little voice. "Mom, are you all right?"

Silence.

16

Johnny tapped on the door. "Mom?"

Another silence, and then a voice said, "Go back to bed, honey." It was a voice Johnny barely recognized, a lifeless, defeated voice.

"I'm scared, Mom. Real scared."

The door opened partway, and Mary O'Brien leaned her head out. Here eyes were red and swollen from crying, her once vibrant face blank as though all the color and life had been sucked out of her. In the dim light, she looked like a frightened little girl in the body of a woman. Mary looked at her son and seemed to recognize his fright. She opened the door, standing there in her pink nightgown with the white lacy pattern below the neckline. "Oh, Johnny," she said as she brought her son into her embrace. Johnny wrapped his arms around her and squeezed. She stroked the back of his neck and said ever so softly, "It will be okay, honey. It will be okay."

When Johnny woke up in the morning, his body felt drained, as if all his energy had escaped overnight. For a moment, he wasn't aware, and then it hit him hard—his father was dead, and his mother had cried alone in her bed last night until Johnny had gone to her. He felt good that he had garnered the courage to get up in the middle of the night and do such a thing. Scared as he was, he did it. And it had seemed to make things a little better for both of them.

*   *   *

The following Tuesday was the funeral. Johnny's mother's sister, Aunt Bess, had arrived from Chicago the day after his father's death and was staying at the house. She was much older than Johnny's mother and seemed more like a grandmother, not only in how old she appeared in her drab, wide-collared black and gray day dress that reminded Johnny of a picture of a Russian peasant in his world geography book, but also in the stiff-upper-lip she cast upon her younger sister, the way a stern mother would look upon a daughter who needed encouragement.

"One thing I learned from Edward's death," Aunt Bess had said to her sister, "is that there is no use in feeling sorry for yourself. You're a widow now, and you must face it head on." Her husband had been British, and the union had given her a bit of a "snooty air," as Johnny had once overheard his mother tell his father.

Aunt Bess took care of all the arrangements with the funeral parlor and the church, and she even took over in the kitchen. She had overcooked a pot roast the previous night that tasted like rawhide. The meal was eaten in silence, other than Aunt Bess reminding her sister of a detail or two about the funeral. "Now remember, Mary, we must be at the church by eight sharp." She had begun to cut her meat and stopped, her sharp-eyed gaze shifting to Johnny. "You, too, young man. No dillydallying."

Afterwards, she shooed her sister from the kitchen. "Mary, I can manage this. Now, off with you. I have the dishes." She was a big help, but Johnny kept thinking how unemotional his aunt was, as if she didn't have a bit of sympathy in her. Her coldhearted efficiency reminded Johnny of Sister Angus Marie, the Mother Superior at his old school. Other than his mother, Aunt Bess was Johnny's last living relative. His father, who grew up in an orphanage, had none that he had known of.

The day began early with his mother laying out Johnny's white shirt, dark-blue tie, and slacks on his bed. "Get dressed quickly, honey," she said as she removed a pair of loafers from his closet, shoes he used to wear every day to Catholic school but now only for Mass on Sunday. "We have to be at the church early."

After dressing, Johnny went into the living room and waited until his mother and aunt emerged, both in black dresses with long sleeves. His mother reminded Johnny of a very sad yet kindly witch. Aunt Bess seemed even sterner looking than usual.

Johnny's aunt drove his father's car, he in the back, his mother sitting dead silent in front. Johnny felt so uncomfortable, saddened by his father's death but at the same time worried about what the future held for him and his mother. Would they have to move?

Would he have to go back to Catholic school? He hated the thought and hated himself for thinking such selfish things on the day his father was being buried.

Johnny had never spoken to his dad about growing up in an orphanage, but it must have been hard. His mind wandered back to his fifth birthday, when his father gave him a horsey ride. What fun to sit on his father's strong, sturdy back and have him bounding around the room whinnying like a horse, Johnny bent down with his little hands wrapped around his father's neck. They were nearly cheek to cheek, his dad's manly scent making Johnny feel so very safe. How great that moment was and how fleeting and short it had been, never to be repeated—Johnny's one horsey ride from his father. It was the only memory of intimacy that Johnny had of his father, while his mother was always hugging him and tucking him in at night and kissing him on the cheek.

"I love you, honey."

"Love you too, Mom."

Johnny wondered why his father never came close to doing such a thing. Maybe he didn't know how to love since he had never had a parent to show how it was done. Maybe he really did love Johnny but didn't know how to say it or show it. He wasn't really sure about that, but that's what he had overheard his mother say to Aunt Bess the previous night. The metallic scraping of the back bumper on the incline into the parking lot broke the thought from Johnny's mind. *Now it begins*, he thought.

Johnny sat in the front pew, crammed between his mother and aunt, surrounded by a sea of somber adults all dressed up, the scent of incense and musty church lingering about. He couldn't wait for this day to be over.

During the service, Johnny's attention drifted in and out as he listened to the eulogies, one by a fellow bowler. "Ed was a quiet man, a fine bowler . . ." The man looked lost as to what else to say. He then shrugged and said, "Lane number six will not be the same on Saturdays without Ed there."

Johnny's father's boss said a few words about what a fine and reliable cartographer Ed O'Brien had been. "Showed up on time, went to his table, and worked."

No one mentioned how much they liked him or what a great guy he was. It was as though his father had been part robot, a man going through the motions of getting himself through a day. "No muss, no fuss" was a phrase Johnny had heard on a TV commercial, a phrase that fit his father.

On the ride to the cemetery, Johnny grieved for not only the loss of his father but also what he had not been able to experience with him—a hug now and then, playing catch, a father-and-son talk about baseball or even bowling. But it was not to be.

*   *   *

Johnny woke up lying on his back, shafts of sunlight peeping between the slats of his bedroom blinds. He had slept deeply, but when he tried to get out of his bed, it seemed as though an anchor was tied to his waist. He struggled up and stood, stretching his arms over his head. Today would be the first day that he and his mother were alone, his aunt having taken a cab to the airport the previous night after the funeral services were finished. The shock of his dad's death had lessened, but in its place was a general feeling of hurt, as though his body had been pummeled from the inside, an achy sense of unhappiness and uncertainty.

Johnny left his room in his red-checked pajamas and found his mother sitting at the dining room table, reading the classified section of the newspaper. "What are you doing, Mom?"

She took one last drag on her cigarette and put it out in a glass ashtray, the scent of her perfume mingling with the smoke. "I'm looking for a job." She was acting calm—too calm—and in that island of tranquility, Johnny smelled fear.

"I want to go back to school today."

"Tomorrow, honey." His mother bit her lower lip and then winced, her eyes two slits, a look Johnny had never seen before. Finally, she said, "We need to talk." She gestured toward a chair at the table, and Johnny took a seat. Johnny prayed she wasn't going to tell him they were going to move. "Your father had a rare heart condition that we were not aware of." She leaned back in her chair and said, "We're going to the hospital today to run some tests on you."

"Ma . . . me?" Johnny stammered. "I don't understand. I'm fine, Mom."

"We need to see if you have inherited your father's condition." She reached over and began to stroke the back of Johnny's neck. "Just want to make sure everything is okay with you." Her tone was light, but behind the false front was a tremor of nerves, a little warble in her voice.

"I don't want to go," Johnny said, shaking his head. "I don't want to know whether I got it or not. I want to go to school today."

Johnny's mother sat back in her chair and said wearily, "No, honey. Now go into your room and get dressed." They exchanged another look, and his mother said, "Please, Johnny, I don't have the strength to argue. Do as I ask. Please."

Johnny turned from his mother and went to his room as ordered. He opened up his dresser drawer and got out his underwear and undershirt. He felt his knees knocking against each other. He plopped down on his bed face first and pulled his knees into his belly as he felt the tears welling in his eyes. He might have his father's illness? How could this be? He was a ten-year-old boy who a few days ago was living a dream life, and now he had lost his father to a bad heart and had to go to a hospital to see if he may have it. And if he did, then what?

Suburban Hospital was less than a mile down Old Georgetown Road from Johnny's house. The sight of the one-story, grayish-white building that Johnny had paid little mind to in the past now had an ominous aura about it, as if there was nothing good he was about to learn inside it.

Much like the day when his father died and the day of the funeral, everything was a blur. First he had to take off his clothes and put on a pale-green hospital gown and flimsy slippers. Then he had his blood drawn by a nurse in one room, and in another he had to stand against a rectangular contraption while a man in a lab coat took pictures from a monitor connected by steel arms to the contraption. Johnny was so scared and felt so all alone. Why wasn't his mother in this room with him? Why did he have to do this?

He then was escorted into a small room with an examination table. After a long, excruciating wait, a tall, angular man in a white doctor's smock entered. He said his name, which Johnny immediately forgot, and then said that he was a cardiologist, a word Johnny was not familiar with. The doctor seemed to read the boy's face and said, "I specialize in people's hearts." After checking his patient over from head to toe, the doctor told Johnny to get dressed and to wait there.

Eventually, a nurse came in, escorted Johnny to a waiting area—the antiseptic smell of the hospital seemingly everywhere—and told him his mother was meeting with the doctor. This was his first time in a hospital other than his birth, and he hated it, hated everything about it and the people inside it. And he hated the secretive things that were going on as he was left sitting all alone.

Finally, his mother arrived with the doctor, and they took Johnny to an office down the corridor. The doctor sat behind a big, imposing desk and explained that Johnny had inherited his father's heart condition. Johnny turned to his mother sitting next to him. "What does it mean, Mom?" She looked at the doctor for help.

"Simply put, Johnny," the doctor said, "you mustn't overexert yourself. No sports and no running. You follow those restrictions, and you may not have a problem until your forties." The doctor placed his elbows on the desk and leaned forward. "There is no known cure for hypertrophic cardio . . ." His voice seemed to disappear into thin air.

"Mom, get me out of here," Johnny said as he stood. "Please, Mom."

On the ride home, Johnny realized that he was not whom he had always thought himself to be: a healthy boy with a love for sports and a flexible, coordinated body. But now he felt flawed. His body had let him down. His heart, of all things, was going to cheat him of a full life. His heart was a ticking time bomb with only so many beats left. How many? How many more beats until it stopped and he died? The thought made his head ache and his body tighten as if a cord had been pulled tight inside his chest, causing him to wonder if his heart might quit on him right now. He remembered the doctor's words: "You may not have a problem to your forties." Could it happen sooner? And even if he made it into his forties, what good was it to live without sports?

Sitting in his mother's car, Johnny was unaware of his surroundings, seeing only what his mind imagined. He saw himself perched on the brick wall at Ayrlawn watching his buddies play ball while he could only sit. No, he couldn't even see himself doing that; it would hurt too much. He wanted to scream at his mother, "I'm going down to Ayrlawn to play ball. If I die, I die." But he couldn't rally the energy to demand anything. He felt so utterly tired and defeated. His life was over, he thought as he came back to the physical world when the car pulled into the driveway.

"Would you like a snack, honey?" Johnny's mother asked as she hung her coat in the hallway closet.

"No, Mom." Johnny handed his mother his jacket. "How can I not play sports? I might as well die right now."

His mother held the jacket against her chest, her eyes glistening for her only child. "Let me make a phone call."

The next day, Johnny didn't go to school. Instead, his mother took him into downtown Bethesda to his regular doctor's office. While his mother waited in the reception area, a nurse escorted Johnny into an examination room and told him to strip down to his underwear. He liked Dr. Fitzgerald a lot, but he was scared. The space felt cold and uninviting, and although not as bad as the hospital, there was some of the same antiseptic smell lingering in the air. Never had he missed more the regular routine of getting up, going to school, and seeing the faces of his friends. It seemed a long time ago.

Shortly after Johnny finished undressing, Dr. Fitzgerald entered. He was an older man who reminded Johnny of a leaner version of Santa Claus without the beard. The doctor put his hand on his young patient's shoulder. "Hello, Johnny," he said in his creaky, singsong voice, a granddad's voice.

The doctor took a seat at a small desk in the corner and went over some papers and X-rays. He looked up, his eyes smiling at Johnny. "Heard you had quite a day for yourself yesterday."

"Yeah," Johnny said, "bad enough I got this heart thing. But now I can't play sports."

"Well, let me take a look at you, and afterward, we'll discuss it with your mother." The doctor secured the stethoscope draped around his neck into his ears and placed the chestpiece over Johnny's heart. It felt cold as ice, shooting a chill down the boy's arms. "How did you like the World Series?" Dr. Fitzgerald asked as he moved the stethoscope around Johnny's chest, as it gradually lost the cold sensation.

"It was good," Johnny said in a ho-hum tone.

The doctor moved around to Johnny's back. "Your Yankees beat my beloved Dodgers."

"Yeah," Johnny said, grinning as his mind began to drift toward baseball rather than why he was there. "We got you back for last year."

After he finished checking Johnny over, Dr. Fitzgerald told him to get dressed and to wait. The nurse then came in and took Johnny to the doctor's office, a cozy space with a row of framed Norman Rockwell paintings from *The Saturday Evening Post* hanging on the pine-paneled walls. One was of boys about Johnny's age in baseball uniforms, gripping the end of a bat to see who hit first.

"Have a seat next to your mother, Johnny," Dr. Fitzgerald said from his high-back leather chair, his hands folded atop his desk. Johnny already felt better being in this good man's company. "I have discussed your situation with your mother," said the doctor. "I want you to come in and see me at the end of each school year. But other than that, I am placing no restrictions on you."

"Does that mean I can play sports?"

"Yes, Johnny." The doctor leaned forward, peering over the top of his wire rim glasses, his eyes fixed on his young patient. "At first you may be a bit hesitant about exerting yourself," he said as he leaned back, tugging his elongated earlobe, "but you may play all the ball you want, me boy."

"What about what the other doctor said?" Immediately, Johnny wished he hadn't asked the question.

"Johnny, I've been in medicine for forty years," Dr. Fitzgerald said as he folded his hands under his chin, his elbows on the desk, "and during that time, I have come to believe that exercise is good for the blood vessels and thus good for the heart." He placed his hand on his chest as if ready to take a pledge of allegiance. "It is my opinion that in your case, no physical exertion would be harmful." The doctor stood and said through a widening grin, "So why don't you get out of here and go outside and play some ball?"

"Play ball? Really?"

Dr. Fitzgerald nodded and said, "Yes, Johnny, really."

On the ride home from the doctor's office, Johnny felt a great relief at being able to play ball, but he was still trying to deal with his bad heart. A bad heart? He peeked over at his mother, who forced a smile. But it wasn't her old smile that seemed to light her face with sunshine; this one couldn't erase the dark cloud that hung over her. An edge of uncertainty lingered in the air between them. His father now dead, Johnny realized how safe his father had made him and his mother feel. Now it was only the two of them.

Johnny wondered if he'd ever feel safe again, for even at his young age, he recognized that he had gone thorough a life-changing series of events: his father's untimely death followed by his life-shortening diagnosis with all its restrictions, only to have Dr. Fitzgerald come to his rescue at the last moment. It reminded Johnny of a movie, only the ending wasn't all that happy, with his father dead and his life getting cut short by a flawed heart.

He stole another peek at his mother, who had a tight, two-fisted grip on the steering wheel as they waited at a stoplight. She looked at Johnny with another halfhearted smile. She almost seemed like a different person. Yes, she still looked like his mother, but she was different. Her face that used to have a constant glow, those bright eyes shining joy, was now replaced by a downward slant at the corner of her eyes and mouth that seemed permanent.

The light turned green, as the car accelerated, his mother said, "I think it best if we keep your heart condition to ourselves."

"That's fine with me." Just then, they passed by Suburban Hospital, its name in bold blue letters atop the entrance overhang. The sight of the hospital registered in Johnny's belly like a body blow. Part of him knew that hospitals did good things and saved lives, but all he got from that one was a life cut in half.

"I don't ever want to go inside a hospital again." His tone was determined yet respectful.

"Neither do I, honey," his mother said as she glanced over at the hospital. "Neither do I."

Chapter 2

A New Beginning

A month after Ed O'Brien's death, Johnny came home from school to something he was still getting used to—an empty house. His mother had gotten a job with a real estate firm in Bethesda as a receptionist/secretary. He got a plate of cheese and saltine crackers his mother had left for him from the fridge and poured himself a glass of milk, but there was no more Ovaltine. "We have to cut costs now, honey," his mother had told him.

Johnny sat in the dining room, eating with a sort of tired vigor. He was still trying to adjust to all the new changes in his life. He tried to tuck his heart condition away in the back of his mind, telling himself that forty seemed like forever, but there was a little worry that was always flitting around in his head that he had a bad heart and was going die before his time.

Johnny took another bite but didn't savor snacks after school like he used to. Besides not having chocolate milk anymore, the cheese and crackers didn't taste as good, as though his taste buds had changed. It seemed as though everything around his house had changed, especially his mother, whose sad expression seemed permanent. Even when she smiled, it wasn't the same old Mom. Her glow seemed gone for good, replaced by the tired and worn-out look of a woman left to fend for herself and her child.

Johnny thought back to a phone call his mother had received from a neighbor a few days back. Mary was helping Johnny at the dinner table with a homework assignment when the phone rang. "I'll get it," she said through a sigh. "Oh, hi, Edith . . . . Oh, cocktail party . . . . No, thank you, Edith. I don't think I can make it," Mary replied in a sad little voice. "I would feel funny there without Ed." When she hung up the phone, Johnny glanced up at his mother for an instant before returning to his book, not able to bear the painful longing in her eyes.

As he finished off his last cracker and washed it down with milk, Johnny thought about how his mother seemed to have no contact with people outside of her work. He couldn't imagine what his life would be without his friends and that great green spread of land at Ayrlawn that seemed almost like a second home, a happier home, a place where he could lose himself in competition.

Johnny went into the kitchen and rinsed out his glass. He was doing a chore that his mother used to insist on doing. "Go off with you, Johnny, and meet your friends," she would say through her brilliant lipstick smile. He hadn't seen that smile since his dad had died.

It was all different now, he thought as he dried his glass with a dish towel. His mom wasn't home to greet him, and his dad was never coming home from work to have a cocktail with his wife before dinner. Even though he had not been close with his father, Johnny missed him greatly, as though a part of himself were missing, a part of his life—the provider, the security blanket. He missed the sound of his father's heavy footsteps, his voice that had a gravelly warble to it—a man's voice, a voice that Johnny had never realized how much he would miss. He even missed being uncomfortable in his father's presence, for there was that pull of attraction about being around him, his dad, the big, quiet, grumpy man who was a creature of routine. How Johnny now missed that routine of having a father. It made him feel incomplete and a bit jealous of his friends with their complete families.

He began to dry his plate, looking outside where the trees had lost their foliage, the branches barren and lonely. Thin strips of clouds hung in the gray sky like dirty-white rags, the sun nowhere to be seen. He put the plate and glass in the cupboard and turned to go outside, but he stopped and looked around the empty house that didn't seem as safe or anywhere near as happy as it used to be.

He realized that his mother was the source of the joy in the house. Even with his dad's dour presence, she had never let it get to her. Rather, she acted as if there were nothing to prevent her from showering big smiles on her son and little winks here and there. She had loved being a housewife and mother with time for coffee and conversation with neighborhood women. But now there wasn't time for any of it, no lounging around in the kitchen, meticulously dicing vegetables for homemade soup or listening to the radio as she leisurely smoked a cigarette and gazed out the window. Now, Mary O'Brien greeted Johnny with a peck on the cheek—"Hello, honey"— and then right into the kitchen, working like a cyclone to throw together a meal for her and her son. No longer was there an easy smile spread across her face, but rather a sad-eyed look of someone whose world had been turned upside down.

Both their worlds had been turned upside down, Johnny thought as he got his sweatshirt out of the closet and slipped it on. He wanted to turn his mind off this subject and look ahead to playing ball with his buddies, but it was hard when he thought of the life his mom now lived. Every Saturday morning, Mary O'Brien got up early and drove to the supermarket for the week's groceries and then back home to scrub the kitchen floor, clean the house, change the bedsheets, and do the laundry. By the time she finished, it was late afternoon, and then she began preparing dinner. Her only time to herself was on Sunday when, after church, she came home and took a long nap on the sofa. Then she started all over again on Monday.

As Johnny closed the front door and was met by a cold, stiff breeze, he thought how his mother had no life at all. Work and more work. When he volunteered to help, she would have none of it. "No, Johnny dear," she always said in a tired yet resilient voice. "You get only one shot at childhood."

*   *   *

Toward the end of fifth grade, Johnny's life revolved around school and playing ball at Ayrlawn, though the first few months after his initial checkup with Dr. Fitzgerald, Johnny had been cautious about exerting himself, remembering the cardiologist's warning. What if he was right? Try as he might not to, Johnny kept waiting for something to happen, as though his chest might explode if he played too hard. So he did everything at a slower pace, not straining too hard for a rebound or a ball going out of bounds.

The boys noticed this, and during a game of three-on-three basketball, Mickey Doyle, who was on the other team, called him out for not hustling after a loose ball. "Johnny," he scolded, "do you only hustle in baseball?"

As Johnny retrieved the basketball, he heard Dr. Fitzgerald's advice warble in his mind—"Play all the ball you want, me boy." Why was he concerned with what the other doctor, whom he didn't even like, had said about overdoing it? Dr. Fitzgerald had told him he had over forty years of experience and that exercise would be good for his heart. So listen to him.

"You're right," Johnny said to Mickey as he returned to the court. He tossed Mickey the ball. "You're out," he said as he assumed the defensive stance with legs spread and arms out to the side.

Mickey dribbled right with Johnny nearly chest to chest. Mickey tried to go in for a layup, but Johnny was right there on top of him. Johnny jumped up with every ounce of energy he had and blocked the taller boy's shot. Shoulder to shoulder, they lunged after the loose ball, Johnny beating Mickey to it, turning in midair and throwing it back to Danny at the foul line. As he let the ball go, Johnny felt as if he had thrown away a fragment of his fear. He had gone all-out to beat a good ballplayer to a ball and had made a strenuous athletic move in getting the ball back to a teammate—and he felt none the worse. How about that?

After that day, Johnny was mostly okay, except those times when he really pushed himself. Later that year, during a pickup game of touch football at Ayrlawn, Johnny started to throw a pass but brought the ball back down as Tip, small but quick, charged toward him with arms raised. Johnny took off to his right, quickly picking up speed, hauling ass down the sideline, gasping for air in the biting cold as he sprinted all the way for a touchdown. When he stopped, he doubled over, his lungs screaming.

He'd been out of breath before, but back then, he had been unaware of his *condition.* He stood in the makeshift end zone of four sticks in the ground, hands on knees, and felt his heart thumping against his chest. Could he die right here? The other kids were calling out "Great run!" and waving for him to come back to the middle of the field.

"Wait," Johnny said with a little wave. His breathing had slowed, as had his heartbeat, but he could still feel it pitter-patter inside him. Time seemed to slow down. *Pit-a-pat, pit-a-pat, pit-a-pat,* went his heart. And then he was good again. His breath was back to normal, and he no longer felt his heartbeat. But a tremor of nerves tingled down his arms as he trotted back. He told himself to remember Dr. Fitzgerald's words that exercise was good for his heart. But still, it was a bit scary to have a heart condition and feel it pounding in his chest, for he processed everything differently now.

CHAPTER 3

THE BROWN'S STORE INCIDENT

Johnny's condition brought about an awareness of not only his own mortality but a sense of responsibility for his boys. He wasn't sure why that was and didn't dwell on it, but he felt as though he were on high alert regarding his five best friends: Brian Lagos, a recent addition, a sturdily built, square-shouldered boy with hooded eyes that had a kind of tranquil look hinting at an even disposition; Brad Harper, the biggest of the boys, with an outgoing, somewhat abrasive personality and a bit of a reckless streak, who liked nothing better than starting a spitball battle in class when the teacher's back was turned; little Tip Durham, a fine-looking kid with mahogany-colored hair and squinty gray eyes that darted from face to face when he talked in a group; Danny McKenzie, Johnny's best friend, a quiet yet determined boy with dirty-blond hair, a pug nose, and a sprinkling of light-brown freckles under each eye; and then there was Mickey Doyle, the lanky, freckle-faced kid with a wiry thrash of hair that was cut close on the sides but rippled with short, defiant curls sprouting on top.

One day after school, Johnny was down at the basketball court at Ayrlawn. "Where's Mickey?" he asked, as there were only four kids.

"He's with Mike Andros," Brian said.

"Oh, no," Tip moaned, "that guy is trouble." His thin lips puckered so that his face had the worried look of a little old man.

"I saw them," Brian said as he lifted his chin in the direction of the little backstop at the far corner of the field and then raised his chin again to indicate further past a line of trees, the wind whistling through their bare branches. "They were on Mike's front porch talking like they had a secret." He bounced the ball once and caught it. "And when they saw me, they stopped." He cocked the ball over his shoulder, flicked his wrist effortlessly, and launched a shot that swished through the metal rim.

"Yeah," Danny said as he retrieved the ball, "I saw them, too." He passed the ball back to Brian. "Mickey tried to act like he didn't see me."

"I don't like Andros," Tip said as he caught Brian's shot that clanged off the rim. "He's always getting Doyle in trouble."

"He's okay," Brad chipped in. "We worked on a science project together. He did just about the whole thing, and we got an A." He wiped his nose with the back of the sleeve of his sweatshirt and said, "My first A."

Johnny and Mike were the two smartest kids in their sixth grade class. Both received straight As. Mike was a whiz in math, even better than Johnny, while Johnny was his equal in other subjects and maybe even a little better in English. There was an unspoken level of respect between the two of them, and neither ever tried to show off their intellect. They were smart and they knew it, but they didn't have to show it. And in Mike's case, he acted the opposite, a little spitfire with a bowlegged gait and a jutting "I dare you" chin. He called himself "the Phantom" and liked to talk out of the side of his mouth, and though small, he would stand up to anybody if challenged. In high school, he would use that aggression as a three-year starter on the varsity wrestling team.

Johnny volunteered to sit out and let the other kids play a game of two-on-two. Halfway through, he saw Mickey scrambling down the hill off Hempstead into a full sprint. The wind had picked up, and he noticed Moo Moo, the weather vane, spinning like a green whirling dervish as if in warning.

Mickey pulled up at the court's edge, his shirt and pockets bulging. "I'm in deep shit," he gasped, hands on knees as he drew deep breaths. The game stopped, and everyone came over to him.

"Whatta you got there?" Tip asked.

Mickey removed a Snickers from his pocket.

"What happened?" said the boys, hovering around the ashen-faced Mickey.

Mickey explained that Mike had a plan that involved him diverting Mrs. Brown away from the front counter while Mickey hit the candy case at Brown's Store. Mike got Mrs. Brown over to the end of the store to make him a sandwich while Mickey began loading up his pockets with Snickers, Mars bars, and the like. "I got carried away and stuffed myself." Mickey jiggled the front of his shirt. "I nearly cleaned out the candy display."

But when he had turned for the door, Mrs. Brown looked up and saw a candy bar fall from Mickey's pockets. "Mickey Doyle, stop right there." Mickey froze for a moment and then bolted for the door. "I am going to call your father, young man," were the last words Mickey heard as he swung open the front door and ran like the devil out of there.

"My old man is going to beat the tar out me, Johnny," Mickey said in a crackling voice.

Brad reached into Mickey's pocket and pulled out a Snickers and a Milky Way. "Free candy," he hooted as he tossed the Snickers to Brian.

"What difference does it make?" Mickey said as he began to empty his pockets, a treasure trove of stolen loot falling on the court. "I'm a dead man anyway."

"Stop," Johnny said. "Brad, Brian, hand the candy back to Mickey. I got an idea." Johnny's tone wasn't bossy but more friendly and persuasive, anticipating a great adventure. Without missing a beat, the two boys handed the candy back to Mickey. Johnny said, "Let's collect all the candy, Mick, and go to your house and get what we need."

"My house?" Mickey cried.

"Just trust me, Mickey. I got an idea."

In Mickey's bedroom, Johnny rifled through the dresser, picking out underwear and undershirts. He went to the closet and took a flannel shirt off the hanger and stuffed the undergarments in it, knotting it tight with the sleeves. "Okay, now we need a long stick."

Mickey sat on the edge of his bed, shaking his head. "Johnny, how is this gonna get me out of trouble?"

"Doesn't your father have an old stick I've seen him walking around the neighborhood with?"

"Yes, but—"

"Where is it?"

"In the closet downstairs, but it was my grandfather's shillelagh. If anything happens to that, I am dead, Johnny. Dead."

Mrs. Doyle was in the kitchen making dinner when the two boys came downstairs. The closet was in the hallway near the front door and out of her line of sight. Johnny opened the door and removed a shiny, knotty stick with a large knob on top. "Perfect," he said.

Brown's was a country store on the corner of Old Georgetown and Greentree. It was a small, clapboard structure that sold sandwiches, basics such as bread and milk, and an inviting display of candy at the front counter. Mrs. Brown was a trusting, kindly woman who reminded one of a youngish grandmother.

On the store's porch, Johnny took an empty milk crate sitting on the Coca-Cola cooler and had Mickey load all the candy into it. He handed Mickey the bundle of clothes on the walking stick and told him to sit there with his back to the store and look dejected. "I don't have to act for that," Mickey said.

Johnny found Mrs. Brown stacking canned goods on a shelf and asked if he could speak with her for a moment at the front counter where he had placed all the candy.

"Oh, I see you ran into Mickey Doyle," Mrs. Brown said evenly.

Mickey glanced at the crate of candy and then turned to Mrs. Brown and said with all the sincerity he could muster, "He's *really* sorry, Mrs. Brown."

"Of course he is. He got caught."

"He's real worried about you calling his dad. He's thinking about running away rather than facing the Belt."

"The belt," Mrs. Brown said, scrunching up her face. "What do you mean, Johnny?"

"His dad will give him a beating if he finds out about this." Johnny tilted his chin toward the crate of candy. "It's all there."

Mrs. Brown looked at the candy, then at Johnny, a question in her eyes. "Beating?" she said with a heightened tone of concern.

"I've seen welts on Mickey's fanny from stuff much less than what he'll get if his father finds out about this." Johnny nodded as if to confirm his words and said, "The whole thing wasn't even Mickey's idea."

"Oh, I figured that," Mrs. Brown said, wagging a finger at Johnny. "That Mike Andros is a sly little devil."

"Really, Mrs. Brown, Mickey is really, truly sorry. I can promise you he will never do anything like this again." Johnny turned his bright blue eyes on Mrs. Brown and smiled his boyishly handsome smile. "He's outside right now and wants to come in and apologize." Johnny's expression turned mildly grave, his lips pursed, eyes beckoning for understanding.

Mrs. Brown looked at Johnny, her front teeth resting on her bottom lip. She shook her head ever so slightly. There was a trace of motherly concern about her, but mingled with it was the pragmatic businesswoman who couldn't allow theft in her store.

"He's already packed some clothes and is going to run away if his father finds out." Johnny brought his hands in front of himself, palms up. "It's in your hands, ma'am."

Mrs. Brown drew back, her eyes still suspicious.

Johnny motioned toward the front window for Mrs. Brown to take a look. She went to the window, and there was Mickey with hobo pack over his slumped shoulder. He looked for all the world like the loneliest of boys.

"Oh, my," Mrs. Brown said, "the poor dear." She studied the scene before her. "Is that his father's walking stick on his shoulder?"

Without missing a beat, Johnny said, "He wants something to remember his family by."

"Goodness gracious," Mrs. Brown said with a sigh, "tell him to come into the store."

Mickey faced Mrs. Brown, who was behind the counter, hands on the carton of pilfered candy. Lanky, wiry Mickey had an expressive face, a face like the map of Ireland, which showed every emotion he was feeling. In this situation, it was a good thing. He was the most pitiful-looking boy, his eyes like saucers, a slight tremble in his lips, and his body twitching as if it had the hiccups.

"I . . . am *sooo* sorry," Mickey said in a raspy whisper. A tear streaked down his cheek from his left eye; the right was clear—one of Mickey's many unique traits. He sighed so heavily that Johnny put his hand on Mickey's shoulder and squeezed.

"All right then, Mickey" Mrs. Brown said. "I think you have learned your lesson."

It was as all downhill after that. For years later, Johnny told the story of how he saved Mickey's ass.

Later that night, lying in his bed, Johnny turned the day's events over in his head. During his rescue of Mickey, Johnny had felt a righteous sense of purpose that involved more than saving a friend. His allegiance was not only to Mickey but also to himself; he had some sort of awareness that he would need his boys for the rest of his life—however long that was to be.

Chapter 4

North Bethesda

By the time Johnny entered seventh grade, he had settled back into a routine of school and sports, his heart condition tucked away in that little corner in the back of his mind. But one sport that he did not participate in was the Pop Warner tackle football team that his friends had joined. His mother wouldn't allow him to play, not only because of his heart but mostly because she worried about him breaking bones or worse. "I've heard about a boy getting paralyzed playing tackle football, Johnny."

"Mom, I'm not gonna get hurt," Johnny replied. He wished his father were alive to let him play. His dad had been the boss in these matters, and it seemed to Johnny his mother was having a problem making a reasonable decision about this.

"You're all I've have," his mother answered in a cracking voice, a voice that begged him not to fight her on this.

Mostly Johnny was upset that he couldn't play, but a small part of him was okay with it, since he feared that a direct hit to his heart might damage it. He had considered asking his mother to check with Dr. Fitzgerald, but he decided to let it pass. It was scary to think about a helmet to his heart. So for the tail end of summer, Danny, Mickey, Tip, Brad, and Brian practiced football at Ayrlawn, and Johnny would either stay home or shoot hoops on the basketball court, mostly by himself or with younger kids. That was hard to do, since he could see and hear the coach on nearly every play blowing the whistle, shouting instructions to the players, followed by the momentary silence before the cracking clap of hands after breaking a huddle. He never walked past the practice on the field, instead taking a longer way home behind the tennis courts through a patch of woods.

The disappointment of not playing football was lessened somewhat by a new phenomenon that had skirted Johnny's horizon. It began at the end of sixth grade, when Johnny and friends began attending parties at girls' houses. He enjoyed dancing to songs such as "At the Hop" by Danny and the Juniors and "Sweet Little Sixteen" by Chuck Berry. The exhilarating beat of the music, the touch, and the sweet girlish scent combined in a confusing rush of desire and fear— desire to be close to a girl and fear from a little voice in Johnny's head that said to be careful, as he was still sorting out his heart condition and all its ramifications. Plus, his Catholic school upbringing had made it clear that any type of intimacy with a girl was a no-no.

Even so, Johnny's interaction with and awareness of girls heightened his first year at North Bethesda Junior High, only a few blocks down Hempstead from his house. He had encountered the school his first day in his new neighborhood but had given it little thought since. The school was only a few years old and was a typical suburban junior high for its time: an L-shaped building with brick exterior, wide hallways with shiny metal lockers, and a combination gym-auditorium. Behind the school was a large grassy area with a backstop and diamond at the far end. The first day of seventh grade was a whirlwind of activity, with so many new faces and pretty girls dressed in their saddle shoes and skirts with white blouses. For the first time, Johnny had a schedule, going from one classroom to the other with a different teacher in each. The school bells that were supposed to go off to indicate the end of class were clanging off whenever they felt like it throughout the morning. Between classes, the hallways buzzed with bells ringing, ratcheting up a jangling excitement as kids scurried about, some totally lost and confused.

At lunch in the cafeteria, Johnny met up with Tip and Danny. They sat at a long table with a group of other seventh graders from Bradmoor Elementary. Johnny knew the names of some of the boys from playing them in Little League over the summer and struck up a conversation with them. By the end of lunch, they had invited Johnny and company out back after school to flip quarters. Johnny wasn't sure how this all worked but figured it had something to do with gambling.

After the last class, Johnny, Tip, and Danny went out back to discover three sets of boys facing each other, flipping quarters and catching them in the air, taking turns yelling out "odd" or "even." They would open their hands simultaneously to reveal two heads, two tails, or a head and a tail. Quarters were exchanging hands at rapid-fire speed. Mike Andros was in one set of boys. He soon cleaned out one kid. "Hah, hah," he said triumphantly. "Better luck next time, sucker." He jutted his chin in Johnny's direction. "Any takers?" he said as he flipped a quarter and snatched it out of the air. "Who wants to lose their lunch money?"

"I'm in," Johnny said as he removed a quarter from his pocket. He went over and faced Andros. "You call first, Mike."

Andros grinned and nodded. "Ready, Johnny boy?"

They flipped and caught their coins. Andros looked at Johnny for a moment, then said, "Even." They removed their top hands to reveal a pair of George Washingtons. "Hah," Andros exclaimed. The Old Phantom was enjoying himself.

Tip and Danny came over for a better look as they flipped again. Johnny said, "Odd." He made a little face at two eagles. "I got one quarter left. Your call, Mike."

"Even," Andros declared. A head and a tails came up. "Damn," Mike said.

This was Johnny's first direct competition with Mike, who rarely played down at Ayrlawn, and it was different in that no athletic skill was involved. Johnny wasn't even sure if any sort of intelligence was required, but that what to call relied more on gut instincts. It seemed Andros was very good at it, and Johnny took the look from Mike when he had said, "Any takers?" as a direct challenge—the two smartest boys going head to head.

They continued to flip, no one winning more than two games in a row. Finally, Andros said, "I'll flip you one time for everything you got."

Johnny shrugged. "Sure. It's my call."

The other kids flipping heard the challenge and came over to watch. The quarters went into the air and slapped down on their palms. Mike squinted at Johnny with a sideways sneer, and Johnny returned the look with his easy smile as if this were no big deal. They continued to eye each other with sly grins of anticipation. They were in the moment, like a pair of actors playing out their script for all it was worth.

"You guys going to show?" Tip said.

"I got to make the call first, Tip," Johnny explained.

"Go on, Johnny boy," Mike said.

"I'll call, and then we'll have a countdown before we show." Johnny looked at Mike, who nodded okay. Johnny was ready to call out *even*, but then he considered that this entire competition was odd, and an *odd* call was the right way to go.

"Odd," Johnny said, still covering his coin, his eyes shining with mischievous gleam, but behind the gleam was a strong desire to take down his cocky adversary.

The onlookers squeezed around the combatants, and Mike said sharply, "Back off, bud." They stepped back, but one kid still had his neck craned so that his head was hovering near Mike's hands. "Hey, you mind?" Mike said.

"Sorry," the boy replied as he straightened up.

"Okay, on three." Andros said "one" and nodded at Johnny to indicate his turn.

"Twoooo," Johnny said.

The Phantom looked around at the circle of kids, cocky as could be. "You dirtbags should have to pay to see this." He looked at Johnny and said, "Three." They showed their hands to reveal a heads for Johnny and a tails for Mike, whose face pinched a little as he said, "Sheeeet."

"That's four quarters, Mikey boy." Johnny stuck out his hand as Andros handed over the change.

It felt great to win at this new form of competition, and it surprised Johnny that he felt so strongly about beating Mike. But on the walk home from school, Danny talked up the Bethesda Colts' first game the upcoming Saturday at Ayrlawn. "I'm going to see some playing time at defensive end, and Brad has nailed down the starting job at center, and Brian . . ." As Danny went on, it crossed Johnny's mind that flipping quarters was no substitute for Pop Warner football. Next year, he decided he would work on his mother and even talk with Dr Fitzgerald if necessary, for he had an ache in his stomach from missing out on something like real competition—tackle football.

But even the boys who played football were finding their attention diverted by parties at girls' homes, where sometimes the parents would leave them alone in a finished basement. One of the girls suggested Spin the Bottle, and Johnny received his first kiss. The lingering touch of her lips on his registered like a cannon shot—*kaboom*—stirring Johnny in a heightened rush of something so new and different and exhilarating that he felt slightly lightheaded.

And then there was another kiss with another girl who, instead of spinning, pointed the bottle boldly at Johnny. She reached over and clutched the back of his neck with her fingers laced and kissed him. "I've been wanting to do that since fifth grade," she said with a startled look of surprise as though her words had not been her own.

Johnny felt his cheeks blush crimson as his head swirled from not only the liquid kiss but also the warm imprint left on his neck. It was all so new.

Seventh grade was when Johnny had turned a corner with girls, but his heart was never far from his mind and the vague uncertainty over how it would affect his interaction with girls in the future. But there was one thing that Johnny was not vague about—his strategy for next year.

BETHESDA COLTS
WASHINGTON BOYS CLUB LEAGUE
1958

Chapter 5

The Bethesda Colts

At the end of the school year, Johnny had his annual checkup with Dr. Fitzgerald. He waited until the completion of the exam, when he had been given the all clear. The doctor was about to leave the room when Johnny made his pitch. "My friends played Pop Warner football last year." Johnny sat on the exam table in his underwear, looking at Dr. Fitzgerald, who sat back down at his table in the corner.

"Ah," he said, nodding. "I played high school football." He nodded again and looked at Johnny with a remembering look. "One of the best experiences of my life."

Johnny leaned forward, palms up. "My mother won't let me play."

"Oh," Dr. Fitzgerald said as he seemed to recognize that Johnny had more to say.

"She's worried about me getting injured," Johnny said. "I'm not worried about that, but—"

"You're worried you might injure your heart." Dr. Fitzgerald leaned back in his chair and balled his hand into a fist and rested his chin on it.

"Yes," Johnny said. "I'm afraid if I got hit in the chest with a helmet"—Johnny shrugged and raised his hands in front of himself—"it might stop beating."

"No," the doctor said, shaking his head. "You are no more likely to get hurt than any other boy."

"Really?" Johnny said as he felt a rush of anticipation.

The doctor scratched under his chin with the back of his hand. "Do you want to play?"

"I really do, Dr. Fitz."

"You get dressed, and I'll talk with your mother." The doctor stood and shined a smile on his patient. "Not to worry, Johnny, me boy, not to worry."

*   *   *

A couple of days before the first practice, the players reported to a storage shed behind the basketball court at Ayrlawn. They received their practice equipment, and the coach, Brad Harper's dad, handed out plays diagrammed on sheets of paper stapled together. "I want these plays for your position memorized by first practice," he said in a stern voice. Johnny was beginning to get butterflies. Although Dr. Fitzgerald said he was as safe as the next boy, still he fretted.

By the first day of practice, Johnny reported to Ayrlawn in his football equipment. It felt strange wearing a helmet and shoulder pads, but the white practice jersey with Bethesda Colts across his chest in baby-blue lettering was about the neatest thing he had ever worn, even though it was raggedy.

The first day of practice, Mr. Harper had all the boys who wanted to play quarterback throw the ball to receivers. Mickey and Johnny were the only candidates, and it was soon evident that not only did Johnny have a more accurate arm, but when they ran a bootleg drill where the quarterback had the option to pass or run, Johnny's agility and speed were also obvious.

Johnny was also telling the linemen where they were to go on plays. "You know the guard's plays, too, Johnny?" Mr. Harper asked as he loomed over the huddle.

"Yes, sir. I memorized all the positions." Mr. Harper rocked back on his feet, his face registering a look of someone coming into good fortune, a coach's look that said, *I got me a ballplayer here.* Mickey was soon shifted to running back, and Johnny assumed the role of team quarterback.

But during the second day of practice, Mr. Harper ran tackling drills where one player had the ball and faced off against another boy who had to tackle him. Ayrlawn echoed with the cracking sound of shoulder pads colliding, boys grunting, and Mr. Harper yelling, "Give it all you have, son, all you have!"

When Johnny's turn came up, he squared off with Brad, the hardest hitter on the team. Brad got down in a three-point stance, and Johnny stood a few yards away gripping the football. Mr. Harper blew the whistle, and Johnny ran into Brad sort of sideways. Brad wrapped his arms around Johnny's waist, lifted him off his feet, and came down on top of him, thumping him to the ground. Johnny felt a quiver of pain in his shoulder, but he was fine. But Mr. Harper stopped practice and told Johnny to hit the tackler square. "This is not a game for the faint of heart." He blew his whistle and ordered them to line up again.

Fair enough, Johnny thought. This time, he ran straight at Brad with everything he had, but Brad rose up and hit Johnny with his shoulder right in the chest, driving him to the ground, landing Johnny flat on his back with the hulking Brad crashing down on top him.

"Great run, great hit," Mr. Harper roared with savage delight.

Brad got off Johnny and offered his hand to help him up. It surprised Johnny that he had taken a direct hit and was none the worse other than a sore spot on his chest. His heart felt no different.

He felt no different. *So*, he thought as he reached for Brad's hand, *maybe I am as safe as the rest of the boys.* But in scrimmages, he still used his speed and shifty moves to avoid as much contact as he could. Why take a chance on his faulty heart?

After two weeks of practice, all the positions were set, and Johnny thought they were a strong team, with Brad and Brian anchoring the line, Mickey and Tip at running back, and Danny at end. They ran a T formation with three backs lined up behind the quarterback.

Mr. Harper ran practice with ruthless efficiency, scaring the bejesus out of all boys. He was a big man, six-four and a lean two-twenty-five that gave the impression of power in reserve. He had been wounded at Guadalcanal and still had the bearing of the Marine First Lieutenant he had been—strict and no-nonsense, and a perfectionist who seemed to miss nothing.

At practice at Ayrlawn, he could call out three players on one play. "McKenzie," he bellowed at Danny and then raised his hands overhead for everything to stop. When he did, everyone stopped. "Son, catch the ball with your hands, not your chest." Without missing a beat, he jabbed a finger at Brad. "Harper." He called his own son by his last name at practice. "Snap that damn ball, and fire out at the linebacker like you mean it." Then he threw his hands out in front of himself in disgust. "And Lagos, *son*." He drew the word out—*suuun.* "Get your fanny down and drive through on your block." It became a term the boys would call each other for years. *Son, what you up to? See you later, son. Son, I say son, how you doin'?*

The one player Mr. Harper never berated was Johnny. On the rare occasion Johnny messed up, the coach would be encouraging. "Johnny, Johnny, fake that pitch like you mean it, son. You can do better." Johnny was the type of kid at whom it didn't seem right or proper to holler at. Besides, he was the leader of the team, and Mr. Harper also seemed sensitive to the fact that Johnny had lost his dad. Johnny even wondered if he knew of his heart condition. Johnny asked his mother, but she denied it.

"Never, Johnny," she had said with conviction. "That is our secret."

A week before the first game, the boys had a hard, tough practice, and afterward, Mr. Harper had them circle around him. "Distribution of game uniforms and weigh-in tomorrow morning at nine sharp at the storage shed." He looked around at the boys until his gaze rested on Tip. "You gonna make weight, Durham?"

"Yes, sir, Mr. Harper," Tip said in a tone that indicated he hoped so. The boys had to weigh a minimum of seventy-five pounds and no more than one-twenty-five. The only kid who had a problem was Tip, who had been eating bananas by the boatload and guzzling milk in an attempt to get up to the required weight.

Heading home, Tip told Johnny that he was three pounds shy and needed somehow to make the weight. "I know what we need to do, Tip," Johnny said. He told Tip to meet him early before the weigh-in.

The following morning, Johnny found Tip pacing back and forth at the little backstop. Tip stopped in his tracks when he saw Johnny toting a pillow case slung over his back. "What's in that, and how is it going help me meet weight?"

Johnny turned the sack upside down, and a pile of rocks rolled out. There were round ones, flat ones, and some in between, but all were less than the size of a baseball. Tip looked at Johnny, then the rocks, and then back at Johnny. He bopped his head and took a quick, sharp breath. "Ah, yeah, Johnny, yeah."

"Stuff one in each front pocket and two in the front of your underpants and a couple of flat ones in your back pockets."

Tip stuffed his pockets first and then his underpants, but his jeans drooped in the crotch. "Oh no," Tip said.

Johnny held up Tip's pants by the belt loops. "Suck it in, and tighten your belt."

Tip took a deep breath and squeezed his belt tight. "Whoa," he gasped. "Those rocks are cold."

The scale was a regular doctor's scale, and a representative from the league would do the weigh-in. Every boy except Johnny had a father there with him. Even Mickey Doyle's father was there. Mickey had told Johnny the only time his father paid attention to him was when he got in trouble.

If only my father were here with me, Johnny thought. The first game was at Ayrlawn, in the afternoon after his dad would have finished his nap. All he would have had to do was walk down the street and watch his son play quarterback for the Bethesda Colts. If only his father had seen him play, Johnny and his dad could have had something to talk about at dinner. "That was a very fine pass you threw in the corner of the end zone, Johnny." Or, "I had no idea my son was such the runner." Or, "Sunday, how about I take you to a Redskins game?" If only.

Johnny stood off on the side, watching some of the fathers and their sons talking in clusters, everyone waiting for the weigh-in to begin. Johnny felt like an outsider as he felt a lump rise in his throat. Oh, how he wished his dad were here at his side.

He was on the verge of crying when he felt a large hand on his shoulder. "Johnny." He looked up to see Mr. Harper, his normally demanding eyes soft and gentle. Johnny had never noticed before how light blue and true they were. "You know I have a tradition of giving the number one to my captain." Mr. Harper rubbed Johnny's shoulder. Johnny nodded, his head swirling from this big bear of a man coming to his rescue, this heroic man who every boy on the team feared and idolized.

"It was an easy choice this year." Mr. Harper smiled, his straight white teeth glistening in the morning sun. He tousled Johnny's hair and said, "Captain Johnny O'Brien has a good ring to it."

"Really?" Johnny said as he felt a surge of pride wash away his moody blues.

Mr. Harper jerked his thumb over toward the scale and said in a pretend strict voice, "Now get over, Cap'n, and lead your team in this weigh-in."

The fathers were in a circle around the scale as each boy came up to be weighed and announced. "Brad Harper, 120 pounds . . . Mickey Doyle, 105 pounds . . ."

Johnny was in line behind Tip, who was twitching about like a little ball of nerves. "Relax, Tip. Everyone here is on your side."

Tip nodded his head, his shoulders still bobbing.

Tip stood on the scale, and the man adjusted the measuring rod: "76½ pounds." Tip let out a stream of air as he turned from the scale, his mouth open in a silent *oh* at the wonder of it all. He leaned his head toward Johnny and whispered, "Thanks."

The first game was against a team from Silver Spring, and the Colts won it going away. Johnny ran for two touchdowns and threw another to Danny on an option play. It was the most fun Johnny had ever had. He lost not only himself in the game but also his fear of getting hit in the chest.

But the next Monday at practice, Mr. Harper was all over the boys. "Doyle, you're running like an old lady. McKenzie, catch with your hands, son, your hands." Mr. Harper stuck his hands, which were the size of frying pans, in Danny's face. "You understand?"

"Yes, sir, Mr. Harper."

The Colts won their first three games. The following week at the end of practice, the team was running wind sprints across the width of Ayrlawn from sideline to sideline, Mr. Harper exhorting them, "Give it all you have, boys, all you have."

Johnny had never lost a sprint, but Mickey was always trying to beat him, lining up next to him and staying with him for the first few steps before Johnny put it into another gear to win going away. "Way to run, son," Mr. Harper would say in a ringing voice. Johnny never tired of receiving the great man's compliments.

"Take a breath, boys," Mr. Harper said as the team was lined in a row on the sideline, their backs to the basketball court. The players were sucking for air, some bent over, hands on knees. The air had a brisk chill to it, but Johnny felt flushed with energy. He looked over Ayrlawn—the stand of trees on the rise next to the big backstop;

the foliage an array of shimmering oranges, reds, and yellows; the once-green field now worn and battered from the constant pounding of cleats; and Moo Moo whirling high and free atop the silo from swirling gusts of wind. How neat it all was.

"All right, boys, everyone give their all," Mr. Harper said as he paced in front of the team, "and we'll call it a day." He was wearing his standard uniform, football cleats and trench coat over his gray flannel suit, reminding Johnny of a general addressing the troops before a battle. Mr. Harper raised his hand and said, "Ready." He blew his whistle, and everyone took off running toward the far sideline.

Johnny could hear Mickey grunting as he ran stride for stride with him. Johnny stuck out his chest and pumped his arms vigorously, pulling away from Mickey. Nearing the sideline, Johnny felt his foot give way as he stepped into a divot and fell as though shot. For a second, he felt nothing until a shooting pain ran up his ankle and up through his leg. "Oww," he shouted as he lay on his side, clutching his ankle.

Mr. Harper rushed over to him as the team surrounded them in hushed silence. "Don't try and get up, son." Mr. Harper helped Johnny to a sitting position, got down on one knee, and carefully pulled down Johnny's knee sock to get a look. He felt Johnny's ankle with his thumb and forefinger.

"Ahh," Johnny said wincing.

"Doesn't appear to be broken, but it's already starting to swell." Mr. Harper stood. "I'll drive you home, and I want you to put ice on it until your doctor gets there."

Johnny was out for the next game, and with Mickey at quarterback, the Colts lost a game against a tough team from Wheaton by a field goal. It had been agonizing for Johnny to stand there on the sidelines, leaning on his crutches as his boys went down in defeat.

But a week after the injury, Johnny felt as good as new. He got the okay from Dr. Fitzgerald, who was amazed by how quickly Johnny recovered. "You're a lighting-quick healer, Johnny me lad."

Johnny returned to practice and was greeted by an ear-to-ear-smile from Mr. Harper. "He's back," the big man said. "I got back my quarterback."

The team won its next three games with Johnny running the offense with exacting precision. The season came down to the last game of the year—Bethesda Colts vs. the Rockville Lions, who were undefeated. The winner of the game would be league champ. For years there had been bad blood between Rockville and Bethesda. Rockville was a hardscrabble town full of tough-guy rednecks. The place had a Southern aura to it. And although only less than ten miles separated Bethesda from its neighbor to the north, it seemed like another world. Rockville kids considered Bethesda a place for spoiled rich kids, and kids from Bethesda considered Rockville a haven for greasers.

The game was played at a park in a little shabby, run-down neighborhood in Rockville, where the homes were similar to Johnny's but smaller. Some were missing siding or a shutter here or there, and the yards were neat but surrounded by chain link fences. Johnny felt as though he were entering enemy territory.

This was more than a game. It was a battle of cultures—rednecks vs. urbanites. There were no bleachers, and the parents of each team stood on their respective sideline. Many of the fathers from both sides had served during WWII, and one would have thought they would not get that excited about a Pop Warner football game. Wrong. They were ready for bear.

Both sides were encouraging the players during warm-ups when one of the Rockville players hooted, "Lookie, lookie. It's the pussy boys from Bethesda." The Rockville fathers got a big kick out of that.

Johnny, who was leading the Colts in jumping jacks, stopped and said, "Hear that? Let's show 'em who we are." The laughter of grown men at the expense of his teammates, his boys from Bethesda, rankled Johnny and made him even more determined to lead his team to victory. He'd show them who they were.

The game was a hard-hitting, head-banging battle from the first whistle to the end. The middle linebacker for the Lions, who had made the pussy boys comment, keyed on Johnny the whole game and hit him whenever he could, talking all while. "You ain't gonna last the game, boy. You look tired, number one."

On one play, the middle linebacker had lowered his shoulder into Johnny's midsection on a quarterback sneak and left Johnny on the ground, gasping for air. "Shit, they got themselves a pansy ass for a quarterback." Johnny struggled to his feet, returned to the huddle, determined to make his nemesis eat his words.

With six seconds left in the game, the Colts had the ball on their own thirty-yard line, down by a score of 21 to 17. Johnny called his last time out and ran to the sidelines to confer with Mr. Harper.

"Johnny," Mr. Harper said as he placed his hands on his quarterback's shoulder pads, "that left outside linebacker has been cheating inside all day." He lowered his head, looking Johnny square in the eyes. "What's the call?"

"Fake a run away from that side, and then run the quarterback keeper."

Mr. Harper straightened up to his full height, his shoulders square, and nodded with an expression of confident assurance. "All right, Cap'n, make me proud."

Johnny trotted back to the huddle, still hearing Mr. Harper's words: "Make me proud." But Johnny had never been so tired, his body one big ache, having played the entire game. He also called all the plays on defense from his safety position. But he could not let Mr. Harper or his boys down. He was determined to make this final play work.

"I'm going to fake a handoff to Mickey sweeping the left end—and sell it, Mick—and then run a bootleg around your end, Danny. The outside linebacker has been cheating inside all day. Drive him toward the middle." Johnny looked around the huddle, all eyes on him. "We can do this. We will do this." He clapped his hands once and said, "On one."

Brad snapped the ball to Johnny, who wheeled around with his back to the line and faked the handoff to Mickey, who then ran like the dickens around the left end, pretending to have the ball tucked in his left arm. The defense reacted for just a second as Johnny swept past Danny—who secured his block on the outside linebacker—like a blur, running up the sideline. He strained with everything he had, his lungs screaming. The middle linebacker recovered quickly and had an angle on Johnny. As he neared, Johnny stopped on a dime and cut back toward the middle of the field, leaving his opponent gasping for air. *How great was that? Not bad for a pussy boy, huh?* He ran with every ounce of energy he could muster toward the end zone, weaving around another helpless Lion who ended up on his backside.

Ten yards from pay dirt, everything seemed to slow down. Johnny's conscious mind was fully engaged with the moment at hand, but in the dark recesses was the lingering thought to savor this moment, to take it all in and remember it for the rest of his life. When he crossed the goal line, everything sped back up, the rumbly eruption of the crowd fast forwarding him. Then he felt a surge of panic as he felt his heart beating as though ready to explode: *Pit-a-pat, pit-a-pat, pit-a-pat.* Gasping for air, he felt a strange sense of victory with death at his doorstep. Then his teammates mobbed him, and Johnny was swallowed by the moment and what he had accomplished, his heart condition shoved back down into that little box in the back of his mind.

As his teammates whooped and screamed, Johnny flashed his brilliant smile from behind his one-bar face mask and said, "We showed them who the boys from Bethesda are."

Mr. Harper came over, lifted Johnny off the ground, and gave him a giant bear hug. To be embraced by a fatherly figure like Mr. Harper gave Johnny an overwhelming sense of approval. His face was buried in the big man's neck, the scent of Old Spice and tobacco wafting in his nostrils—what a moment.

Mr. Harper put his hands on Johnny's shoulder pads. "You got heart, Johnny, a big heart, son."

Chapter 6

Bethesda Hot Shoppes

After three raucous years at North Bethesda Junior High, the boys entered Walter Johnson High School. Even toward the end of twelfth grade, Johnny had maintained a bond with his core group of buddies from Ayrlawn. Danny McKenzie, his best friend, had grown into a big baby-faced kid and standout pitcher on the baseball team. Mickey Doyle was a bigger version of the freckle-faced boy Johnny had first met. Brad Harper was nearly his father's size and a standout football player. Tip Durham was still the smallest of the group and the wittiest, save Johnny. And Brian Lagos had developed into a top-notch wrestler by combining deceiving strength with quick reflexes. All the boys other than Tip played on the high school football team, but things had been somewhat fragmented by some of the boys spending time with girlfriends, especially Brian and Brad, who had dated steadies since junior year.

Johnny dated in high school but was still attempting to sort out his heart condition and all its ramifications in his relationship with the opposite sex. What would happen if he told a girl? Would she walk away from him? Be sympathetic? But even if she was, wouldn't she consider him flawed and eventually want to move on to a guy with a full life ahead of him? Part of him wanted to share his secret with a girl, but that little voice in his head told him *not yet*; plus, there was his mother's advice to keep it to himself, and he trusted her judgment.

So Johnny kept his secret from his two girlfriends during high school. The first was a shy girl who was outside the mainstream of popular kids whom Johnny hung with. Barbara Livingstone had short black hair and dark brown eyes that bespoke intelligence, and in her gaze there was something gentle, soft, and quiet. She wasn't gorgeous but had more a look of refined beauty. Johnny and Barbara had met in junior English lit class. What drew Johnny's attention was her knowledge of literature, and though she was not a big talker in class, when she spoke, it was always something relevant. Johnny asked her out, and though there was a look of anticipation in her eyes, at first she hesitated. "I don't think I fit in with your friends," she had replied.

"Let's go to a movie, just the two of us, and see how it goes." Johnny's tone was low-key and calm.

Soon they were going downtown to catch a Saturday matinee to watch a French movie with subtitles, or to picnic at Great Falls, or sometimes to visit a museum downtown in DC. Barbara had opened up a new world that was quiet and thoughtful and different in a good sort of way. Johnny was balancing time with her and his mach-speed world of jocks. She was a level-headed girl with a wide array of interests, from literature to history to baseball. "I love the way Willie Mays plays center field," she told Johnny one time during a break from studying together for an exam. "His basket catch is almost a form of art." Both were virgins, and Johnny never pushed it too far. Barbara enjoyed necking, but if Johnny went for her breasts, her body tightened like a knotted cord as she brought her arms across her chest.

At the end of junior year, Barbara's father transferred out of state, and though part of Johnny missed her, another part was relieved to have his freedom back. Not that he felt trapped, but sometimes he felt obligated to spend time with her when Danny, Mickey, and Tip were heading out to a party, boys out on their own. There was also a certain relief regarding his heart condition—he no longer felt guilty about not telling her, as though his representation of himself as the hale and hearty athlete was a big lie.

Johnny's second girlfriend was Betsy Monroe, who was the complete opposite of Barbara Livingstone: honey-blond hair with an outgoing personality and curvy figure that she wasn't afraid to show off, wearing tight sweaters and low-cut skirts that highlighted her shapely legs. During her first two years at WJ, she had dated a boy a grade ahead, and when he went off to college, she set her sights on handsome Johnny O'Brien, the star quarterback with the winning personality. She was the head cheerleader, and during senior year at the first football game of the season at WJ, she led a cheer. "Johnny, Johnny, he's our man. If he can't do it, no one can. Go Spartans."

After the game that WJ won, she sidled up to Johnny as he made his way toward the locker room, receiving slaps on the shoulder pads and congrats from his teammates. She grabbed his forearm and squeezed. "You were great today, Johnny." She looked up at Johnny with stardust in her eyes and flashed a smile that reminded him of a Pepsodent commercial.

"Thank you, Betsy."

She asked him if he was going to a party at one of the cheerleaders' house later that evening.

"I will if you go with me," Johnny said as he raised his hand to some classmates who were yelling, "Great game, Johnny."

From then on, they were a couple, Johnny drawn to her bombshell body and she to the star quarterback. From the beginning, he realized how superficial their relationship was. But she was a beautiful girl, and Johnny was a red-blooded American boy. They had heavy-duty makeout sessions, but her lower half was off limits.

Johnny found this out in the back seat at a drive-in when he finally got up the nerve and placed his hand on her thigh. She removed it and placed it on her firm, ample breast. "Here is where that goes," she said.

As much as Betsy flaunted her physical attributes, she was adamant about no sex. "I'm saving that for my husband." By the end of football season, Betsy wanted to be with him all the time on weekends and was jealous of Johnny talking to other girls at school. By this point, he really missed his quiet times with Barbara and their discussions about things outside of the high school social scene.

So one Friday, instead of picking her up at her place at seven, he called to tell her he was going out with Danny and Tip.

"Johnny O'Brien," she sputtered in a hostile tone, "would you rather be with them than me?"

"Betsy," Johnny said, "maybe it's best if we—"

"Save your breath, Johnny O'Brien. It was nice knowing you."

As the whamming rattle of her phoned slammed in his ear, Johnny realized he had a lot to learn about girls. He also realized that he had not felt as guilty about not sharing his heart situation with Betsy since the relationship was more physical than platonic. He imagined her reaction if he had told her of a pouty face and a one word reply: "Ooh." In any event, Johnny needed to get back to hanging with his buddies, and the place to do that during senior year was the drive-in at Hot Shoppes on Friday nights, right in the heart of downtown Bethesda on Wisconsin Avenue.

Bethesda Hot Shoppes was a one-story structure with a low-slung shingled roof and a glass front with a stained wood trim and stone façade. Along the front and sides was a parking lot and in the back a concrete island with parking spaces along both lengths, each equipped with a microphone to order food from carhops dressed in snappy uniforms with bow ties and side caps atop their heads. The carhops would zip around balancing platters of Mighty Mos—the original Big Mac—fries, and shakes, trying to avoid collisions with hepped-up kids infected with Friday night fever. By seven thirty, the parking spots were full of carloads of high schoolers, while the inside was packed with older folks and families with children.

Kids from the three local high schools—WJ, Bethesda Chevy Chase (or BCC, as it was called) and Walt Whitman—congregated at the car hop island, and Johnny acted as a go-between, having secured friendships with the various factions from each school. He had made friends with such characters as Corky Espinoza, a charismatic hood from Cabin John, and Bo Connors, the burly, tough-guy president of the Lourdes from BCC. With a rippled thicket of jet-black hair, striking dark blue eyes, and a finely cut, easygoing handsomeness, whatever *it* was, Johnny had it. He had worked the previous two summers as a counselor at the Jelleff Boys Club—reuniting with the Dillon brothers, who were big-time football players at St. Johns High in DC—and had saved up enough money to buy a '54 Ford from a neighbor who gave him a break on the price. Danny hadn't gotten around to getting his license, so he was usually found riding shotgun in the Gray Ghost, as the boys called it.

Something was always bound to happen at Shoppes—maybe a fight behind Grand Union right next to the drive-in, or a convertible filled with pretty girls from Whitman arriving and parking right next to them, or even a hot-rodder zipping in and popping the hood for all to gawk at his powerful engine.

Shoppes was a place where kids found out about parties. The best were in Potomac in horse country, where the parents were rich and lenient. Beer often flowed at these noisy gatherings, and on occasion a fight would break out. One such incident was in the springtime of senior year at Happy Borger's house, a huge split-level out off Falls Road near Great Falls in an exclusive neighborhood with horses grazing in corralled yards. Johnny, Mickey, and Danny were in attendance. On the back patio, where a keg was set up, they greeted some acquaintances from Whitman's football team. Johnny always liked the Whitman kids, who were friendly and loved to party. The other half of the party was in the living room off the patio, where a buffet table was set up with pretzels and chips and dip, nothing fancy. Danny and Mickey had already tapped beers from the keg, but Johnny held off. Dr. Fitzgerald had warned him about being careful with his intake of alcohol, and besides, he was perfectly content if he didn't drink.

About an hour into the party, Danny was feeling no pain. Normally shy to the core around girls, he was having a grand time talking with a cute girl from Whitman on the patio. Before Danny knew it, she had led him inside to a hallway, where she wrapped her arms around his waist and started kissing him. Johnny caught all this from a sofa in the living room. He was feeling a bit under the weather, with low energy and a general tiredness, something rare for Johnny, who, despite his heart condition, never got sick.

Out of the blue, Johnny saw an older guy lunge at Danny and punch him right in the jaw. This wild man in his twenties started laying into him, but Danny was a big boy by this time, nearly two hundred pounds, and threw the jerk off of him. Johnny rushed over with some kids from Whitman and held the aggressor back.

"Hold on, Crazy Jimmy," Dave Hodge, the fullback on the Whitman team, demanded while he had an iron-clad grip around the crazy man's chest.

"You're gonna die, boy," Crazy Jimmy screamed at Danny through slobbering lips. "You done barked up the wrong tree, pilgrim." Crazy Jimmy was wearing raggedy jeans with a wide black belt holding an assortment of keys on a chain and a white T-shirt with a pack of cigarettes rolled up the sleeve. He even had a tattoo of an anchor on his forearm, looking for all the world like some wild-eyed man-child. His hair was cut close to the sides, but on top was a wild tangle that swept down his forehead over large, saucerlike eyes that seemed to whirl in no discernible pattern. His pugnacious greaser face was all twisted up in a sideways sneer. "Let me go, goddamn it." Seemingly already past his physical peak, as though he had aged in dog years, he struggled halfheartedly to get at Danny. It seemed the girl flirting with Danny was Crazy Jimmy's girlfriend—he twenty-five and she all of sixteen. Finally, Jimmy calmed down and staggered off with his girlfriend, arms around each other's waists. There went Danny's romance for the night.

David Hodge told Danny and Johnny that Jimmy had been in the navy and had been in and out of the loony bin during his military tour. "He's crazy, but once you get to know him, he's an okay guy." David laughed and said to Danny, "He probably won't even remember you by tomorrow."

Danny shook his head, trying to make sense with what just happened. "That would be fine with me, Dave."

Later, one of Crazy Jimmy's little underlings, a punk kid from Travilah—the poor section of Potomac where the parents scratched out a living, many working as grooms or laborers at the big horse farms—started giving Danny a mouthful of lip as they were ready to drive off in the Gray Ghost. Punk boy had a beer in one hand and a cigarette in the other and was egging Danny on in a loud, abrasive tone. Johnny noted a neighbor coming out to see what all the noise was about. Danny, riding shotgun, told Johnny to stop the car, but instead, he picked up speed. "We've had enough excitement for one night, Danny."

Danny started to open the door. Johnny reached over with his right hand and grabbed Danny by the collar, jerking him away from the door.

"Johnny, we can't let that little twerp get away with that," Mickey said as he leaned forward from the back, his arms resting on top of the front seat.

"Turn around," Danny demanded. But Johnny kept on driving.

A few blocks from the party, they came to a stop sign. Danny opened the door and was halfway out when two cop cars with lights whirling and sirens blaring came barreling past them.

"Still want to fight that kid, Danny?" Johnny said as he motioned Danny back inside. He slowly accelerated. "Timing is everything boys—everything."

"Let's go to Shoppes," Mickey said. "The night is still young."

Johnny was feeling tired, very tired, with a splitting headache to boot. But he didn't want to let his friends down. "Why not?" he said.

Back at Shoppes, they ran into some kids from BCC who told them about another party. Johnny and Danny weren't interested, but Mickey piled into a car, and off he went. Johnny and Danny went inside to the bathroom, where a redheaded kid with a face littered with splotchy freckles like rust spots stormed in and started giving them a boatload of grief. He was obviously drunk. Johnny ignored him and started to leave but stopped. "Don't do anything stupid, Danny," he said before he began to feel lightheaded. "Danny, come on."

Danny was going eyeball to eyeball with Freckles and said, "Just a minute, Johnny."

"Right now, Danny," Johnny said in a faint voice before the room began to spin.

When Johnny woke up, he was stretched out on the bathroom floor with two men from the Bethesda Rescue Squad dressed in the same white uniforms that he had seen the day of his father's death. A cold chill like a hollow shudder ransacked Johnny's body. "I'm okay," he said as he tried to sit up, but one of the men kept a hand on his chest.

"Stay down until we check you out." The man felt Johnny's forehead with the back of his hand and then put his fingertips on Johnny's wrist. "How old are you, son?"

"Eighteen," Johnny answered as he looked around to find Danny standing over him. The other kid was gone.

The man then took a stethoscope from a black bag and checked out Johnny's chest. "We need to get you to Suburban Hospital for further tests."

"What's wrong?"

"You have a fever, but more than that, you have a heart murmur."

Johnny exchanged a look with a shock-faced Danny before he sat up. "No Suburban," he said as memories of his last time there with the cardiologist came to the front of his mind. "But I will see my doctor first thing tomorrow. I promise."

"Can't make you go," the man said. "You're an adult now."

On the ride home, Danny kept looking over at Johnny, the Gray Ghost driving in and out of the shadows, the interior of the car illuminated for a moment by an overhead streetlight before returning to the darkness. Finally, when they came to the stoplight at Suburban Hospital, Danny said, "Shouldn't you go to the hospital, Johnny?"

Johnny looked over at the hospital swathed in light from the inside and out, reminding him of something otherworldly. Something to be avoided. Part of him wanted to share his secret with his best friend, but instead he said, "No," in a flat voice as the light turned green and he began to accelerate.

As they came to a red light in front of Brown's Store, Danny said, "A heart murmur sounds scary, Johnny."

Johnny kept his eyes straight ahead. His head felt as though it were being pounded by tiny hammers from the inside. He wanted to get home and into his bed. "Johnny," Danny said, "what's going on?"

Johnny looked over at his friend, and even in the muted light, he saw the outline of concern in his tight lips and eyes crowded in thought. He wanted to say something to alleviate Danny's concern, but the truth of it was, he didn't know what to tell him. Danny was right—a heart murmur did sound scary. But he would not set foot inside Suburban. He would wait until tomorrow to visit the kindly and reassuring Dr. Fitzgerald.

That night, sleep was hard to come by for Johnny. He kept thinking that maybe his heart condition had accelerated and this was the first sign of an early death. He tossed and turned, and when he did sleep, he had a terrible dream that he was on an operating table at Suburban Hospital, and that horrible cardiologist was getting ready to cut open his chest. "This might hurt a little, young man," the doctor said in a toneless, uncaring voice as he sharpened the blades of a pair of scalpels against each other, the metallic *ping* growing louder and louder until Johnny awoke in a cold sweat, crossing his hands in front of his face as he mumbled, "No, no." He got out of bed and changed his sweat-soaked T-shirt, and it crossed his mind that he hadn't felt this frightened since his one real visit to the hospital.

The next morning, Johnny felt weak and had no appetite. He had looked up *heart murmur* in the encyclopedia and found that it was an extra or unusual sound during a heartbeat. The strange thing was that he never got sick. Heart condition or not, he had never missed a day of school, other than when his father had died. He was old enough now to see the irony of the situation. He called Doctor Fitzgerald's office first thing Saturday and made an appointment for later that morning. He didn't want to worry his mother and told her he was going to the library for a school assignment.

Johnny sat in Dr. Fitzgerald's examination room in his underwear. He turned his head at the click of the door opening. The doctor entered, dressed in slacks and a short-sleeved white medical coat. "Johnny, me boy." The doctor placed his hand on Johnny's shoulder, his warm touch soothing the young man's nerves. Dr. Fitzgerald sat at his desk in the corner and said, "So, I hear you had a bit of an incident."

Johnny explained what had happened the night before, and the doctor listened patiently. When Johnny finished, Dr Fitzgerald said, "Well, let me look you over and see what we have." After a thorough exam, including his throat, the doctor returned to his desk, folded his arms across his chest, and nodded. "You do have a heart murmur, Johnny, but you have had it since you first came to see me. It's harmless." He glanced at Johnny for a second and said, "You do have strep throat, though." He shrugged as if it were no big deal. "I'll write you a prescription, and you'll be good as new in a few days."

"That's it?" Johnny said. "Strep throat?" He breathed a sigh of relief. "Wow, I was really worried that it was something bad."

A thin, pragmatic smile creased the doctor's lips as he removed the prescription pad from his coat pocket. It was a smile that Johnny had come to know that meant everything was going to be okay. It was always okay with Dr. Fitzgerald. "Now," the doctor said as he tore off Johnny's prescription and handed it to him, "get this filled and go home and rest. No ball, no parties." The doctor sat back in his chair and said in a changed voice, "A couple other things, Johnny." Dr. Fitzgerald paused for a moment and then said, "I'll be retiring at the end of the year."

"What?"

"I'm going to sell the practice to a young fellow." Doctor Fitzgerald seemed to read Johnny's face and what he was thinking. "You should continue to come in for an annual, Johnny."

There were a million things Johnny wanted to say to that kindly, wonderful man, but he only nodded and said, "Uh-huh."

"The last thing," the doctor said as he opened the desk drawer and removed a folder, "is that you have a thorough understanding of your situation." The doctor lifted the folder as though displaying exhibit A. "Inside is a copy of a medical paper from the *New England Journal of Medicine* on your heart condition."

Johnny felt a knot in his gut swell up to his throat. "I don't want to know what it says."

"Do you respect me, Johnny?" Doctor Fitzgerald cocked his head off to the side, his raised brow demanding an answer.

"You know I do, Dr. Fitz."

"Then you are going to listen to me. During your childhood, I protected you from the nitty-gritty details in regard to your heart. But you're eighteen now. You're an adult." The doctor squinted hard at Johnny and said, "I am going to explain to you what's inside here." He tapped his index finger on the manila folder. "You have a genetic anomaly in your body by which you are missing a gene that controls . . ."

Johnny listened intently as the doctor broke down in layman's terms the role that genes play in the body and how his lack of one little gene was causing his heart muscle to thicken. He explained that his condition was extremely rare and with no hope for a cure in Johnny's lifetime. "As your body ages," the doctor said, "you become more susceptible."

In the doctor's pale eyes, Johnny saw sympathy. "So there's nothing I can really do, then, is there?"

Dr. Fitzgerald raised a cautionary finger. "Yes, there is," he said. "It's important that you maintain a healthy diet, exercise regularly, and," the doctor said, drawing the word out, "as I've told you, be moderate in your consumption of alcohol."

"I pretty much do all that now, Dr. Fitz."

"Then you may well live longer than your father, who was a smoker and didn't exercise."

"Or I may not?"

"Could be," the doctor said in a tone that indicated, *but probably not.*

"But in the end," Johnny said, "it's going to get me. Right?"

"Yes, Johnny, that is correct," the doctor said, nodding. "And finally, if you have children, there's a fifty-fifty chance you will pass it on to them."

"Wow," Johnny said with an air of finality. "Wow."

On the drive back home, Johnny thought about everything Dr. Fitzgerald had told him. None of it seemed fair. Dying young he had come to terms with to some degree, but to learn that he could pass it on to his children seemed cruel. He had never given much thought to getting married and raising a family, but now he didn't see how he could possibly do such a thing. First off, why marry someone if you're going to die on them? And then how could you possibly have children if you could pass this curse on to them? Life was not fair.

Back home, Johnny found his mother in the backyard tending to her vegetable garden in a back corner that received sufficient sunlight. The yard was a secluded, crescent-shaped spot overlooking Ayrlawn with formidable evergreen shrubs on one side and on the other a thicket of trees. "Hey, Mom."

Johnny's mother turned from pruning a tomato plant. "Hello, honey." At forty-five years old, Mary O'Brien's face had a melancholy beauty with soft blue eyes that expressed a sort of joyful sadness. The once perfectly formed chin had a bit of excess beneath it, as did her figure, which had expanded even more into heavyset middle age. She had been a widow for eight years, all of which she had worked as a secretary for the real estate firm in Bethesda. It seemed to Johnny that her life revolved around him, her house, and her work. She put a pair of scissors in the front pocket of her kitchen apron, seeming to sense something was going on.

"I went and saw Dr. Fitzgerald."

"Oh," his mother said. "Your physical isn't until next month."

"I've got strep throat. I didn't want to worry you."

Her eyes crinkled at the corners as she smiled understandably. "What did Dr. Fitzgerald have to say?"

"Did you know that I can pass *it* on to my children?"

"Yes, I knew." She stood before her son for a moment with an expectant slant to her eyebrows. "I hope you are not upset with me."

"No, Mom," Johnny said, shaking his head. "I could never be upset with you." He looked at the yellow flowers on the tomato plants, the little green fruits just emerging. "I should have figured it out anyway, but it seemed easier not to think about it."

Mary nodded and looked at Johnny. "How did the rest of the checkup go?"

"I'm okay," Johnny said with some weariness in his voice. "But Dr. Fitzgerald is retiring."

"Oh," she said cautiously as she studied her son's face, as though she too were reading his thoughts.

"I'm done with doctors, Mom." Johnny drew a deep breath and exhaled.

"You're all I have left," his mother said in a quivering voice as her eyes seemed on the brink of bursting into tears. Johnny went to her, and they embraced, her fingers desperately pressing into the small of Johnny's back as he inhaled her scent of earth and feminine motherly sweat, flashing him back to the day his father died as she held her little boy tight in her arms.

Johnny leaned back, holding his mother by the arms. "Please understand, Mom."

"Oh, Johnny, honey," Mary said with a bleat of helplessness in her voice. She took a breath and sighed as though resigning herself to the situation. "You've grown into a man, a very handsome man," Mary said as she slid her hand to the back of Johnny's neck. "And right before my eyes." She then turned from Johnny and back to her garden.

Johnny called Danny and told him his doctor had said the heart murmur was harmless. "Oh," Danny said in an unconvinced tone. "That's good, I guess." Johnny had considered sharing his condition with Danny, but something that he couldn't put into words told him to hold up. He also told himself he didn't want to burden his friend.

In bed that night, Johnny lay with hands clasped behind his head, wrestling with not only the possibly of passing on his flawed genes to future generations, but also his shortened life span. He most likely didn't have to worry about it until he hit forty, which seemed very far away. But it nagged him, this ticking uncertainty of a heart of his. He told himself to think positively, and then he thought of *carpe diem,* a phrase he had recently learned in Latin class—seize the day.

CHAPTER 7

SO LONG, WJ

On the last Friday of the school year, Danny and Johnny had just pulled into Shoppes when a group of Rockville greasers in their late teens and early twenties roared in, some of the passengers leaning their heads out the window, giving out bad looks and bad vibrations. They were driving loud, souped-up cars around the island, revving their engines, forming a closed chain of front grille to bumper so that no other cars could park or exit.

These guys were older and not to be taken lightly, for rumor had it they carried switchblades and who knew what else. Corky Espinosa and Steve Newman were standing on the island, watching with their bad boy smirks. Johnny affectionately called them and their buddies "the desperados." This duo pushed the envelope with any form of adult authority: fighting, crashing parties, picking up hookers on Fourteenth Street in DC. You name it, and they had probably already done it.

Corky was wearing his drinking lid cocked over his left eye, a madras short-sleeve shirt, jeans with a crease down the middle of each pant leg, and penny loafers with no socks. While he appraised the situation in a cool, detached manner, Newman was getting himself worked up. "Who do these assholes think they are, huh?" he said in a loud, aggravated tone.

"They got the numbers right now, Dude," Corky said. Ole Cork was a pretty good scrapper in his own right, but was cagey and never got into something without good backup. When a bunch of his buddies from Cabin John arrived—back then, Cabin John was like a mini-West Virginia, packed with dirt-tough folks with dirt-tough children—Corky made his move. He snatched a half-finished bottle of Coke from one of his backups, chugged it down, and fired it at the lead car, a baby-blue '57 Chevy, banging a dent in one of the nifty fins in the back.

The procession came to a screeching halt as the rednecks emerged from their vehicles. There were about fifteen in all. For the most part, they were short but lean and muscular, with even a few tattoos. Crazy Jimmy would have fit right in with this crowd. They inspected the back of the lead car for damage. The guy driving the Chevy, who wore his dark hair slicked back in a ducktail, looked over at Corky and his crew. "You gutless punks think you're bad?"

Nobody said a word until Corky yelled out, "Meets us at the football field at WJ. We'll show you how bad we are, asshole."

"Done," the ducktail said. He started to turn toward his car and stopped, pointing a finger right at Corky. "Make sure your chicken-shit ass shows up. I got something special for you, boy." His razor-sharp voice had an ominous, deadly tone. He then got in his car and screeched off, leaving a patch of rubber and his buddies behind him, their hot rods rumbling away and squealing onto Wisconsin Avenue heading north.

Kids began piling into their cars, hooting and screaming in voices that sounded a bit too brave. Johnny was never much for fighting. Actually, he had never been in a fight, but this was a chance to experience something new, something dangerous. He had promised himself to live life for all it was worth, and now was an opportunity to follow through. "Let's go, Danny," Johnny said, "and kick some redneck ass."

"What?"

"Come on," Johnny said as he hustled into his car.

"All right, then."

Johnny backed up, stopped, and put the car back in its parking spot. Danny said, "What are you doing?"

"I can't do it like this," Johnny said, mostly to himself.

"What are you talking about?"

Johnny got out of the car and said, "Got to stop this." He leaned in the open window and looked at Danny. "Somebody could get hurt bad, real bad. Come on," he said, "follow me." They took off running, shooting across traffic on East West Highway, hustled up a block on Wisconsin Avenue, and then left on Montgomery Avenue and to the Montgomery County police station.

The police had always represented something to avoid, a group whose sole purpose was to break up a party or give tickets for speeding or maybe hassle a kid because he was a kid and had no power. But this time, Johnny needed their help.

Johnny and Danny stood across the counter from an officer sitting at a desk in a crisp beige uniform with a black insignia patch on the sleeve and a shining gold badge on his chest. He wore a black holster on his hip, the polished brown handle of his revolver exposed.

Everything about him represented adult authority and power. "Yes, what is it?" the officer said.

"There's going to be a big rumble at the WJ football field." Johnny said.

The officer got up from his desk and came over. He placed his hands on the counter and said, "This better not be a prank."

"Guys from Rockville," Johnny said. "Greasers looking for trouble." He jerked his finger over his shoulder. "It started at Shoppes."

The officer looked at Johnny for a second before his face twisted into a wrinkle of anger. "Damn punks," he said. He went to the two-way radio on his desk and dispatched a squad of patrol cars to the football field.

Danny and Johnny returned to Shoppes. A while later, Corky and Newman arrived, and they immediately held court in the middle of the island. "Some of those greasers were carrying iron chains," Newman said, his face registering the humming eagerness of having participated in a big event.

"That's right, Dude," Corky said. "Them old boys weren't messing around." He tugged at the brim of his drinking lid, a sort of a floppy fedora that might have looked silly on anyone else, but not Corky. "The lead dog in the '57 Chevy," Corky said, cocking his head off to the side and flashing a crooked grin, "was coming toward me with a bowie knife when the cops showed up with lights flashing and sirens blasting." Corky shot a glance at the circle of kids around him, who were hanging on his every word. He was like Robin Hood with his band of Merry Men.

"Yeah, man," Steve added, "when the cops showed, all hell broke loose, everybody running every which way."

Corky nodded, his gaze drifting over to Johnny. "I figure someone must've called the cops." Johnny kept his best poker face, but he saw that Corky knew. Corky nodded with affirmation at Johnny. "Whoever it was saved my ass."

"No shit, Cork," Steve said. "That ducktailed greaser was getting ready to carve you up."

"Yeah," Corky said as he nodded his chin in a slow, steady beat, his gaze on Johnny. "I owe someone a thank you."

Johnny tipped his head ever so slightly toward Corky as he considered what would have happened if he had hauled ass over to the football field at WJ instead of the police station. He needed to reevaluate his definition of *carpe diem*. He was still going to seize the day, but at the same time, he must stay true to who he was.

Some of the kids departed Shoppes, seemingly having had enough excitement for one night, but Danny said, "What now, Johnny? It's still early."

"Something's bound to come up," Johnny said as he saw a red Cadillac convertible with the top down lap the carhop station. In it were Larry Rivers and Kenny Bonner, a couple of party animals from Whitman. Bonner's dad owned a car dealership, and Kenny showed up at Shoppes in a different new car every couple months. And these two never went anywhere without plenty of beer stashed in the trunk. Larry was leaning over the passenger door, hand over head, twirling his finger in the air and hollering out like a celebratory town crier, "Party hearty, Tara Road! Party hearty, Tara Road!"

Johnny waved for them to stop. "What's going on, Larry?"

"We found a dead end street, empty, no houses or anything out off River Road."

Johnny grinned and said, "What are we waiting for?"

The word was passed around, and carloads of boys and even some girls took off for the Potomac Woods. When the caravan stopped at a traffic light at Goldsboro Road, Rivers got out, went to the trunk, and handed a six-pack to Danny riding shotgun in the Gray Ghost. "Wouldn't want you guys getting thirsty." He winked like a member of a secret club before returning to the convertible then hopping over the front door and into his seat. That Larry Rivers was a smooth operator.

Tara Road was a newly paved asphalt street way out in Potomac with nary a house in sight. There were grade stakes in the ground and a few trees had been cut down, a perfect place to make all the noise one wanted without an adult in earshot or getting hassled by the cops. Dude Newman, with Corky riding shotgun, arrived in Dude's baby-blue Corvair convertible with a record player installed under his dashboard playing "Louie Louie." He turned it on full blast, and the party began—twenty or so boys and girls, all without a care in the world, shouting laughing, hooting, making noise just because they could.

Then out of nowhere, a light emerged from up the street, and then the light was rotating and flashing—oh no, not the cops. Kids started running for the woods. Bonner and Rivers jumped in the Caddie with Johnny scurrying into the backseat as they tore off into the woods. Kenny was a good guy, built like a bull and with a happy-go-lucky demeanor—he truly lived to party. He was weaving between giant oak trees and smashing anything else in his path. The ground was soft from a recent rain, but somehow they didn't get stuck. They came to a creek with a three-foot bank, and even Bonner wasn't crazy enough to try and cross it. Kenny cut the engine and turned to Larry. "What now?"

Larry raised his head and said, "Do you hear that?"

"Yeah," Johnny said. "Kids laughing."

"Back it up real careful, Kenny," Larry said. "I think I know what happened."

Kenny put the car in reverse, and the tires began to spin.

"Hold up, Ken," Larry said as he hustled to the trunk, broke up the two cardboard boxes holding the beer, and placed them under the rear tires. "Come on, Johnny," Larry said, motioning to the front of the car. He told Kenny to put it in reverse and accelerate nice and easy while he and Johnny rocked it back and forth. "And then you gotta turn it hard," Larry said, rotating his finger in a circle, "and then hit the gas out of here."

Kenny offered a two-fingered salute. "Whenever you're ready, captain."

The creek was three feet to the rear, and Johnny prayed Kenny didn't rock the car and him and Larry into it. The ground they were standing on was bare and muddy. Farther up there was some wild grass and ground cover that hopefully would provide better traction. Larry and Johnny put their hands on the grill, and Kenny gave it a little gas. They got the car up to a pretty good rocking routine, and then Larry shouted, "Cut it hard, and we'll give it all we have." Larry and Johnny pushed, the Caddie whining its displeasure. The car swerved backward, coming to a stop parallel to the creek. "Halfway there," Larry said as he picked up the mucky cardboard sheets and secured them under the back tires. "All right, Kenny, give her some gas, and we'll push."

Kenny raised a hand over his head, screamed "yee haw," and then floored it.

Larry and Johnny got showered with mud from their black Chucks up to their necks, but the Caddie sidewinded its way onto more stable ground. Larry wiped a gob of muck off his brow. "Old lead-foot Bonner did it again."

When they arrived back at Tara Road, they were greeted with hoots and laughter. Dave Hodge's Pontiac station wagon was parked in the middle of the road with a flashing light he had attached to the roof. He hollered in a booming, leather-lunged voice at Larry, "Damn, didn't mean to scare off the guys with all the beer." He looked them over for a sec and said, "Rivers, were you and Johnny wrestling with Moolah the Mud Wrestler?"

Larry grinned his rakish grin, went to the trunk, and waved everyone over. "The Tara Road Bar is officially open." Everyone broke into laughter at getting away with something. *What a night*, Johnny thought as Larry handed him a beer. They tapped cans. "Let the good times roll," Larry said with a nod of approval.

Standing there listening to the happy chatter at this hideout under the foliage of the tall trees of Tara Road, Johnny wondered how many more utterly carefree evenings such as this he had left before he had to face the responsibilities of adulthood and his ever-present condition.

CHAPTER 8

OCEAN CITY

Beach week was a local tradition when, the week after graduation, many of the seniors from the high schools in the DC area invaded Ocean City, Maryland. Tip had worked the previous summer at a diner on the boardwalk as a dishwasher, and the rest of the boys had been a time or two, either with their families for a week or the weekend jaunt that Brad had organized the previous year, which Johnny missed because of his summer job at Jelleff Boys Club.

Johnny and the boys made the three-hour drive in Brian's Volkswagen van. Brad had made the arrangements for a motel, and when the van pulled into the driveway, Johnny could only smile at the neon sign flashing The Bird's Nest—the *i* and *e* were unlit—a ramshackle row of one-story rooms that backed up to the bay.

Brad jumped out of the backseat, spread his arms out, and crowed, "Let the games begin."

The boys waited outside in the parking lot as Brad checked in, the brackish, dead-fish smell of the bay lingering in the air. The proprietor was an older man with a three-day growth of beard and stub of a cigar clamped in the corner of his mouth. He took a long, careful look at Brad and then peered out the plate glass window to the parking lot. The boys, standing there, hoped the old man wasn't having second thoughts about renting to them. Finally, the proprietor handed Brad the key but wagged a finger as the big guy listened and nodded his head.

When Brad came outside, Johnny asked him what the talk was all about.

"Said he remembered me from last year and didn't want another loud ruckus late at night in the parking lot." Brad twisted his face in self-mocking delight. "Good luck with that, old timer."

The room was nothing more than a bare twelve-by-twelve space with no furniture, other than two bunk beds wedged in a corner, and a dingy bathroom with a shower so tiny that Johnny wondered if Brad could even fit into it. Johnny tossed his sleeping bag on the concrete floor, which was peeling gray paint, and said, "Methinks this fine establishment is more than any gent could ask for." The boys broke up in laughter, and Johnny added, "Like you said, Brad, let the games begin."

The boys traveled light: sleeping bag and a couple of changes of clothes consisting of clean T-shirts, underwear, and a bathing suit, all packed in pillowcases, except Tip, who had a gym bag. Mickey scooted out, returned with his pillowcase packed with ice, and chilled two cases of Pabst on the shower floor. Johnny felt as if he were at the beginning of a great adventure, with his boys no less. He felt free. Something about being away from home seemed to put distance between him and fretting about his heart condition.

After they'd had a few beers in the room, it was starting to get dark outside, and the boys decided to drive to the Ocean City boardwalk, right on the Atlantic Ocean. This was the first time Johnny had ever seen the ocean, which was glistening a blue-black glaze under a fat yellow moon that seemed close enough to reach up and touch. The roar and crash of waves hitting the beach sent a charge through Johnny, a feeling that he was in a different world from back home. He couldn't remember ever feeling so good about himself. Then he remembered the day he came home from playing baseball all day at Ayrlawn. He had been happy-tired—the best day ever—before he discovered his father dead, his happiness plunging into disaster. He didn't consider himself superstitious, but he reminded himself to keep an even keel about things.

They strolled down the boardwalk jam-packed with high school kids and ran into some classmates and a few friends from BCC and Whitman. It was like a great outdoor party without beer. There was an electric excitement up and down the length of the boardwalk with everyone in a grand mood, a week at the beach, and high school classes in your rearview mirror—what more could you ask for?

They ran into Corky Espinoza and Steve Newman, both of whom were growing stubbly beards. "We got jobs at Frontier Town," Corky said, as he reached in his back pocket did a quick count of the boys and handed Johnny six free passes. Corky didn't say anything else, but his expression told Johnny it was a thank you for back at Shoppes.

Meanwhile, Mickey and Dude Newman were eyeballing each other. Their mutual dislike had begun at the start of tenth grade when there was supposed to be a rumble on the football field between North Bethesda and Kensington Junior High. The whole thing was a made-up, bogus event, since most of the kids from both sides got along fine—that is, except for Newman and Doyle, who had not liked each other from the get-go. When Mickey had come up the bleacher steps, Newman was waiting at the top, and *wham*! He hit Mickey right under the eye, a ring on his finger leaving what would become a scar. Mickey had gotten up and was about to launch into Newman when Mr. Anderson, the gym teacher, showed up and broke everything up. They hadn't fought since, but there was always tension in the air when these two were in each other's company.

Brian asked what their jobs were, and Corky said, "You have to show up to find out." He tilted his head toward Steve. "Ain't that right, Dude?"

Before Newman could answer, Brad asked if there were any parties. "We haven't heard anything," Steve replied.

Corky then said they had dates with girls they had met on the beach earlier and had to go. The boys moved on down the boardwalk, but not before Mickey shot one last glare at Dude Newman, who didn't catch it or ignored it.

They walked to the end of the boardwalk and played pinball in an arcade for a while. They then got some boardwalk fries and subs and took a seat on a couple of benches with the ocean at their back. The sub was great, but Johnny was blown away by the fresh-cut vinegary fries, which combined with the brisk salty air seemed to ramp up his appetite.

After eating, they approached an open-air bar on the boardwalk with a line to get in. Inside, a loud band was playing "Good Golly Miss Molly." Most of the customers looked to be college age. Some were dancing and gyrating to the music, yelling over each other in a sweaty froth of carnal joy. The girls were tan and achingly good-looking, wearing shorts and red tank tops. Johnny felt a pang of lust as they shimmied their fannies and swayed their golden-brown shoulders to the music.

"Lifeguards," Tip said, lifting his chin toward the dance floor. "I went to a party of theirs last year."

"Let's see if we can get in," Mickey said.

The boys all looked at each other before Brad said, "What have we got to lose?"

They waited in line for about ten minutes. All the while, Johnny couldn't take his eyes off the girls dancing. Something about the salty air and the breeze and the freedom he felt was shooting a wild surge of wanting to let loose, to drink too many beers and hustle up on the dance floor and show those sexy girls how to really dance.

When they got to the front of the line, the bouncer would have none of it. "You guys aren't anywhere near twenty-one," he said. "I don't care what type of ID you got." He was an older guy dressed in sandals and shorts, somewhere in his mid-twenties, who had the squinty look of someone who had been through a difficult ordeal, a man left standing at the station as the train of life had passed him by. He was ruggedly handsome, a beer-and-a-shot sort of man, with broad shoulders and a tapered waist. His arms were long and sinewy, his muscles like corded knots. Johnny noted a jagged scar across his knee and wondered if it was the source of his going-through-the-motions demeanor. "Your best bet is to find a party, or if you can't find one," the bouncer said through a gap-toothed smirk, "drink a cold beer where you're staying." He lifted his crag of a chin at the boys as though to say, *That is all.* There was something about the finality to his tone and confidence in his grown-man physicality that caused the boys to turn without a further word, like a no-nonsense teacher dismissing class. Even Brad, who normally took an incident like this as a challenge, remained silent.

"You know who that was?" Brian said with a trace of awe in his voice.

"Who?" Mickey said.

"Ray Bender," Brian said as he turned to take one last look at the man. "All-American wrestler at Maryland who had a good shot at making the Olympic team but tore his knee up."

"He's been a lifeguard for the last few years down here," Tip said.

"How'd he hurt his knee?" Johnny asked.

They were walking down the boardwalk, which was pretty much empty. "Got drunk at a party and tried to impress a girl by lifting up the rear end of a car, and his knee gave out." Brian slowed his pace and looked at Johnny. "Dropped out of college, went into a deep funk, and still hasn't gotten out of it."

"Damn," Johnny said. "Damn."

On the ride back to the motel, Mickey, who was sitting in the third row of the van next to Tip, reached in the cooler in the rear and grabbed a couple of iced beers. "Those chicks in that bar were so fine."

"More than fine," Danny said as he reached back from the middle row and took a cold one from Mickey, who then leaned forward to offer Johnny a beer.

"I'll pass for now," Johnny said, as he heard not only Dr. Fitzgerald's cautionary voice but also saw the image of the bouncer, studly Ray Bender, who would regret for the rest of his life having gotten drunk and ripping up his knee. Johnny had something even more valuable to protect—his heart.

Cold beers were distributed and chug-a-lugged as everyone started talking at once about the girls in the bar, shouting and screaming and trying to one-up one another. "Could you imagine having sex with one of those lifeguard chicks?" Danny said as he crushed his empty in his hands.

"You wouldn't know what to do with it," Brad said, turning from the front passenger seat. "Doyle, another brewskie."

Mickey handed the beer to Danny, who offered it to Brad and then pulled back. "And you would know what to do?"

"Give me the damn beer," Brad said in a half-kidding, half-serious growl.

"Brad and Brian are experienced men," Tip piped in from the back. "Been dating the same chickadees for what seems a lifetime. They would most certainly know what to do with those dancing mermaids."

Johnny, Mickey, and Danny laughed uproariously as Brad turned and scrunched his face up into a mock sneer. "Son, I say son," he said as he glanced at Brian behind the wheel, then back, "is that any way to talk about our girls?" His voice was a dead-on imitation of his father, and Johnny saw the son in the father, the handsome, manly face. For a fleeting moment, he wondered if anyone would have seen any of his father in him had his dad lived.

By the time they arrived at the motel, which had only a smattering of cars in the parking lot, the boys had worked themselves into a loud frenzy, emerging from the van shouting and screaming over each other.

A light was on in the office, and the proprietor stormed out when Danny screamed above the fray, mimicking a beer vendor at Senator games. "Cold beer. Get your ice-cold beer here, brother. Cold beer. Get . . ."

"I just threw a group out of here for excessive noise." The old man pulled his stogie from his mouth, flicked an ash, and scratched his stubbly chin. "Want to make it a twofer?" He took a pull on his cigar and blew a gust of smoke out the side of his mouth, his eyes daring the boys to make a move.

"We haven't done anything," Brad said in a challenging tone.

"You," the old man said accusingly, "are lucky I even let your ass back in here."

Even in the dimly lit parking lot, Johnny could see the back of Brad's neck redden. "We'll be no problem, sir." Johnny stepped forward, his hands open in a conciliatory fashion. "Won't we, boys?" Johnny said as he turned, his eyes pegged on Brad. The rest of guys were watching, waiting for Johnny to spin his charm on this cantankerous geezer.

Johnny turned back to the proprietor. "I promise you, sir, there will be no more disturbances."

The old man was sizing Johnny up with a flinty look. "Do you, now?"

"Yes, sir. We recently graduated high school and are going inside to discuss our plans for the rest of our lives." Johnny's tone was utterly sincere, his stance straight and respectable.

The old man took a slow, thoughtful drag on his cigar, his gaze softening.

"I give you my word, sir, there will be no problems from us tonight." Johnny turned back to the boys. "Will there?"

"No, sir," the boys said in unison.

The old man took a short drag on his cigar. A thin smile creased his lips, a congenial smile. "All right." He turned from them and then stopped, his sharp gaze on Brad. "But if I so much as hear a peep"— he jerked his thumb over his shoulder—"you're outta here."

Their room was lit by a bowl-shaped overhead light fixture, the light splaying down in a soft glow, giving the room an otherworldly effect. Brian and Mickey were sitting on the top bunk, unopened beers in hand, bare feet dangling over the edge. The rest of the boys were sitting on their sleeping bags in a circle, legs crossed or knees to chest, like Indians ready to pass the peace pipe.

Tip opened a Pabst with a metal beer can opener hanging around his neck on a string. *Man's best friend,* he called it. "We need to keep Johnny's promise to the old guy." He removed the opener from his neck and handed it to Brad.

"We'll keep it down," Brad said as he tapped his fingers on the lid of his beer, cracked it open, and handed the opener to Danny who then passed it on to Johnny.

Johnny opened his beer and said to Tip, "I said it more as BS to the old guy."

"I know that, but don't you ever think how the rest of your life *is* going to turn out?"

The boys fell into a moment of reflective silence before Danny said, "I want to pitch in the big leagues." He looked around as though expecting to be ribbed, but there was nothing. He took a long pull on his beer and shrugged. "It's been my dream since I threw a curve ball in tryouts at WJ and the coach told me it was special." Danny took another peek at his friends and said, "Funny, from that moment on, I knew I was good at something."

"I want to be a high school teacher," Brian said from up top. "Coach the wrestling team."

"I don't have a clue what I want to do," Mickey said as he caught the opener that Johnny tossed up to him.

"Me, neither," Tip said as he reached up, his back to the bed, and took the opener from Brian and returned it around his neck. "I guess I'll figure it out after college." He looked over at Brad. "What about you, big boy?"

"I just wanna get through college." Brad ran his finger over the rim of his beer can. He took a short swig, his expression that of one seeing someplace faraway. "But I thought that I might become a businessman like my dad."

"Really?" Brian said as though he didn't quite believe it.

"Brad would be good at that," Johnny said with conviction. "People like you, Brad, and you got the tenacity and guts to sell yourself to others."

Johnny shot a look at Brian and then around the circle, his gaze settling on Danny, who said, "I agree." He then said, "What about you, Johnny?"

Johnny felt every eye in the room on him, everyone expecting him to talk about some formulated plan for greatness. Part of him wanted to say, *Boys, I got a bad deal in this life, a bad ticker that can take me any time after forty. What's the use?*

"Johnny," Mickey said in a way that caused Johnny to look up at him. "You can be anything you want and be successful at it. Anything."

Johnny was the first to wake, curled up in his sleeping bag in a corner of the room. A dream came clear in his mind. It was of himself as a father with a boy in a backyard, throwing a baseball. "Like this son," Johnny said as he gripped the ball with two fingers across the seams. The boy looked like Johnny but was taller and broader in the shoulders. But it was his son, all right, with the same infectious smile.

"Like this, Dad?"

"Yes, Junior, that's it."

"Johnny Junior." The words rolled quietly off Johnny's tongue as he felt a strong tug of emotion, as though he had lost something near and dear.

He shook the thought from his head and stood, carefully stepping over Tip, who was asleep on top of his sleeping bag, his gym bag stuffed with clothes as a pillow. He was lying on his back, his hands folded on his chest. Johnny leaned down to check the watch on Tip's wrist and saw that it was nine. He peeked out the slats of the blinds of the casement window, the sky a rich blue. A perfect day lay ahead.

The wheeze of gentle snores came from the top bunk where Brian slept and Mickey down below. Danny and Brad were stretched out across the middle of the floor in sleeping bags like a couple of bears in hibernation. There were empty beer cans everywhere, and the faint smell of puke lingered in the air. Last night, Danny had drank a few too many and had thrown up in the sink. Everyone had drank a few too many, even Johnny, who had downed a grand total of five beers. Too much, but it had been such a good night, not only the introspective talk about their future plans but a trip down memory lane late into the evening, including the Colts and Mr. Harper. "Son, I say son, give it all you have," Brad had said, mimicking the strong-clipped cadence of Mr. Harper's voice, again breaking up the boys. They couldn't get enough of it, Danny wiping a tear from his eye from laughing so hard.

They talked about Ayrlawn, and Mickey mentioned the first day Johnny had arrived. "I was jealous of you at first. Always considered myself as good as any baseball player at Ayrlawn." Mickey paused for a moment and then said, "You were so damn good, but you made it impossible not to like you." They rehashed Mickey's run-in with Tip's cousin, the Brown's Store incident, and then onward to junior high.

"Best time of my life," Tip said. "Never forget when you cleaned out Mike Andros flipping quarters." By the time they called it a night, most of two cases of beer had been drunk, and sleep came quickly to one and all.

Last night was special, Johnny thought as he slipped into his shorts, wishing he could bottle this moment and hold it in time forever. Part of him felt like Peter Pan, not wanting to grow up and face the inevitable, to stay a kid forever or start all over again, again, and again—bad heart and all the rest of it. In this room were his best friends, all with two parents, all with healthy bodies, all with a future that held no limitations, nothing holding them back but themselves. He told himself to stop feeling sorry for himself, that he was here to lose himself in the moment. "Oh, yeah," Johnny said under his breath as he checked his pocket for the six tickets that Corky had given him.

"Come on, boys," Johnny brayed in a sing-songy voice. "We got us free tickets. We're riding the ten o'clock stagecoach at Frontier Town."

He was met by groans and Mickey pleading, "No, please, no. My head is killing me."

But Johnny was relentless in getting them up—singing off key, telling bad jokes with an Irish brogue, and challenging their manhood. "Son, I say son, you need to play hurt today." So up and off they went, half-asleep and bleary-eyed.

Johnny was curious about Corky's and Steve's jobs at Frontier Town, but he figured they would run into them at some point. The place was a make-believe Western town with all the bells and whistles: saloon, blacksmith, bank, gunfights on Main Street, and the stagecoach ride on dirt trails that the boys boarded, with Brad and Brian riding up top with the driver. The ride in the cab was bumpy and dusty, but the creaks and groans of the rattling stagecoach made Johnny think about all the old Westerns he used to love to watch as a kid at the Hiser Theater in downtown Bethesda.

The stage came to a sudden halt, nearly tossing Tip and Mickey into Danny and Johnny as they sat facing each other. "Hands up, dudes." Johnny knew those voices. He looked out from the cab, and there, bigger than life on a pair of horses—big horses—their stubbly beards only adding to their desperado look, sat Corky and Steve. They were dressed in complete cowboy outfits with authentic-looking holsters and guns.

"Are you shitting me?" Mickey said as he got a look at Newman. When the two faux robbers emptied the stagecoach while ordering everyone to get their hands up, Mickey was eyeballing Newman with hands on hips.

"I said get your hands up," Newman barked at Mickey, who stood his ground. The rest of the boys went along with the charade and had their hands up, laughing.

"Hey, outlaw," Johnny said to Corky, "didn't I run into you at Shoppes?"

"Shoppes?" Corky said incredulously. "This is 1876 in Tombstone, Arizona. There ain't no Shoppes."

Meanwhile, Mickey and Steve were glaring at each other, toe to toe, and when Newman shoved Mickey, that was all Mickey needed to tear into Dude with haymaker after haymaker. Nearly three years of pent-up frustration was being unleashed on old Dude Newman, who was a pretty good duker, scrappy, with surprising strength for someone who never participated in any physical activity other than fighting. But Doyle's rage was carrying the day. He had gotten Newman down on the ground and in a headlock when the thunderous clomp of hooves and the creaky rumble of wheels jolted everyone's attention. The stage disappeared around the bend, the driver holding the reins in a death grip, screaming, "Heeelp."

In the confusion, Newman broke away from Mickey, scrambled over to his horse, and mounted up. Corky offered a three-finger salute to the boys. "Another day at the office, gents." An experienced horseman having worked summers at the Potomac Polo Club for years, Corky hopped onto his mount from the rear, reined back so that the horse's front legs lifted up, and hollered, "Hi-yo, Silver!" Very cool. Corky was very cool. He and Dude, who had a few scratches and bruises on his face, rode off around the bend as if on cue. There they galloped off, the two desperados.

The boys rode back to the Bird's Nest hooting and hollering, Mickey gleeful. "I finally wiped that smirk off Newman's face."

"Son, you gave it all you had," Johnny cracked. "Suuun," he said, drawing the word out. Danny laughed so hard, Tip had to pound his back.

*   *   *

That afternoon, the boys hit the beach dressed in their bathing suits, with no towels and little money, the rent to the Bird's Nest and beer having put a major dent in their finances. They stood at the back of the beach near the boardwalk, checking out the scene.

The sun was out, the air had a salty, beachy freshness—so different from the stagnant smell at the motel—and the rolling waves crashing and pounding on the shore shot showers of mist into the air. Girls were everywhere, sunbathing and eyeballing boys as they strutted by, checking them over. It reminded Johnny of Shoppes on a bigger, more invigorating scale.

Johnny elbowed Danny. "Look at that those girls on the big blanket."

"Yeah," Danny said, "they're cute."

"And there are six of them—perfect," Mickey said.

They stood there for a moment trying to figure their next move when Johnny said, "Follow my lead, boys."

As they approached, one of the girls, a pretty blond, looked up from reading a book, showing a right little smile.

"Hi there," Johnny said.

"Hi to you," the girl said, as friendly as could be. The others girls, who had been sunbathing, sat up and honed in on this hunky collection of male youth.

Soon the boys were sitting on the blanket, Johnny paired off with the blond and the others still in that feeling-out period, talking more to the group than an individual.

"You boys hungry?" one of the girls asked.

"We're *always* hungry," Brad said.

The girl smiled at Brad, opened a cooler, and handed out Cokes and sandwiches to the boys. All the while, the boys and girls exchanged information on hometowns. Like the boys, the girls had recently graduated high school. They were from a hardscrabble town in Pennsylvania and seemed less pretentious than the girls back home.

"You girls going to college?" Mickey asked.

The girls looked at each other with a gritty slant in their eyes that said hard times lay ahead. "No," the blond said, "I hope to get a secretarial position with the state government in Harrisburg."

"Oh," Mickey said, the word seeming to hang in the air, as a truth had been revealed—these boys and girls were from different worlds.

"College is overrated," Johnny said through a laugh. "Now, who wants to take a dip in the ocean?"

"Ah, Johnny," Mickey said, "the water's too cold, *waaay* too cold."

He nodded at the girl he was sitting next to for confirmation, but she turned to Mickey and said, "Are you a wimp?"

The guys broke into peals of laughter. Brian Lagos laughed so hard, he began to cough.

"No," Mickey said in a wounded voice. "I was thinking it might be too cold for you girls."

The blond sitting next to Johnny, wearing a red two-piece swimsuit, stood and pretended she was digging. "You're getting yourself in deeper." She then ran for the ocean and dived into the curl of a large breaker right before it pounded on the shore. She bobbed out of the water, turned, and waved. "Everyone, come on in. The water's great." Her girlfriends looked at each other and then the boys.

At the water's edge, Mickey stuck his toe in and grimaced. "Yikes."

Brian wrapped his arms around Mickey's waist, hoisted him off the ground like he was a feather, hauled him into the ocean, and dunked him. Mickey popped up, his face one big, cold cringe. Everybody else jumped in, splashing and screaming.

Later, the girl with Johnny, Betty, said to him, "Why don't you and your buddies come to our place for a cookout?" She said it loud enough for everyone to hear.

Johnny glanced around at the boys, who all had a look of anticipation of something good around the corner. "We'd love to." He looked at Betty, who was on the big-boned side with a wide, petulant face—a good-looking girl, rather stunning in her red two-piece. She looked back at him with a gleam of confidence as if saying, *This one will do me just fine.* Johnny sensed that he might possibly get lucky tonight.

Betty asked him about his plans after college, and Johnny shrugged and looked off at the ocean shimmering blue-green in afternoon light. "I take each day as it comes," he said. He turned back to Betty and smiled his charming smile. "That suit looks great on you." He smiled again and saw in her eyes a look of someone much older. It was a knowing look.

Before heading over to the girls' beach house, they'd had to wait for Mickey to get ready and then were delayed further when he searched for his wallet, which he had forgotten he had hidden under his mattress.

When they parked the VW van in front, Betty was waiting at the front door. The beach house was two blocks from the ocean, a clapboard cottage with siding peeling white paint and an out-of-square, decrepit-looking screened-in front porch.

She told them the rest of the girls were still getting dressed. She escorted them through the sparsely furnished combo living room—dining room with a Formica table in a corner and four rickety cane chairs, past the galleylike kitchen with splotchy green linoleum, and out to the backyard, with a cracked concrete patio and two wrought iron tables and chairs peeling black paint. There was an old metallic grill with a bag of charcoal nearby.

The other girls soon emerged out back, dressed in short shorts or cutoffs and T-shirts. Most seemed to have applied makeup to their eyes, but Betty hadn't. Her blond hair was cut above the shoulders, parted down the middle, and held in place on the sides by bobby pins. She stood confidently on her long, tanned legs, which could have been formed on a lathe, looking for all the world like a honey-gold goddess.

One of the girls ran an electric cord from the kitchen onto the patio and plugged in a clock radio. She turned on a rock-and-roll station, and "Under the Boardwalk" by the Drifters came on—let the party begin. It was a perfect matching, six boys and six girls, all eighteen or soon to turn. At the beach, Brian and Brad had also each paired off with a girl in that casual beach way—nothing too serious, with an underlying understanding from the boys' insouciant air that there were no strings attached, the conversation light and forgettable.

Betty, try as she might to resist, was drawn to Johnny, and they were a striking couple: the handsome lad with the dark, wavy locks and sparkling smile, and the pretty girl with hair of gold. Brad had paired off with the girl who had handed out the sandwiches and afterward rubbed suntan lotion on his back, a short, perky brunette who brought to mind a cheerleader. With him heading off to a college on a full ride in football, they seemed right for each other. Brian had moved in on a quiet, fine-figured girl with dark, curly hair and big brown eyes.

Mickey, Tip, and Danny were wallowing in shyness regarding the remaining three girls. After a few beers, Mickey made his move and started chatting up one of the girls. That left Danny and Tip and two other girls without partners. One of the unspoken-for girls, a redhead with a twinkle in her eyes, said, "You two gonna stand there all day or come over here and talk to us?"

Tip and Danny looked at each other for a moment, and then Tip said, "Sure."

That broke the ice, and the party began. Brian helped the girl he was with get the fire started on the grill, and Tip and Danny helped their girls bring out platters of burgers and hot dogs and bags of chips. Betty and Johnny disappeared into the kitchen and emerged with a bowl of potato salad and coleslaw that she had made earlier. Johnny and Betty set the table with plastic silverware and plates, like a cookout parents might have. It briefly crossed Johnny's mind that these girls were light years ahead of him and his boys.

Just when Brian was getting ready to put the dogs and burgers on the grill, a group of guys appeared from around the side of the house. They were darker than the boys, older-looking, with five o'clock shadows and that same hard edge as the girls but more so. Betty said through tight lips as if her parade were about to be rained on, "Russ, what are you guys doing here?"

The biggest guy, standing in the middle of a row they had formed like soldiers in formation, said, "The mine shut down early today. Thought we'd pay you girls a visit."

"How'd you find out where we were?" Betty said in a simmering tone.

"Your mom," he said as though she already knew the answer. "She said you'd be glad to see us." Russ scanned the boys standing amongst the girls, who had all leaned closer to a boy from Bethesda as if for protection.

Brad, courageous to a fault, stepped forward. He was dressed in cutoffs and a white T-shirt, looking huge like his father and built like an oak tree with massive, thick arms from hours of weightlifting. His youthful appearance was offset by a masculine countenance, the chin, large and deeply cleft, thrust out like a male lion defending his pride. His size and muscle gave the guys from PA pause as they looked him over cautiously. Danny, who was the second biggest of the boys, came up to Brad's side, followed by the rest, save Johnny, who remained back surveying the situation, his gaze steady and sure, his body relaxed and loose, vibrating positive energy.

Russ glanced over the boys, smirked, and then said to Betty, "Looks like we're in time for dinner." He folded his arms across his chest. He was around six feet and heavyset, but not fat. This guy appeared strong and formidable.

Betty strode right up to Russ. "If you cause any trouble—"

"Now, now," Johnny cut in as he stepped in next to Betty. "You fellas drove all the way from PA. I bet you could use a cold one." Johnny nodded and grinned, his charm undeniable. "What do you say?"

A hint of a smile creased the bottom corner of Russ's lips, and without missing a beat, Johnny said, "I'm Johnny O'Brien, your server for the evening." He did a little dance. "A bit of entertainment, me Irish jiggly wig," Johnny said as he kicked his feet out left and right in quick, short paces, his shoulders swaying in perfect rhythm. He then bowed with hand across waist and swept his hands out in front of him. "At your service, sir." Johnny then launched back into his Irish jiggly wig, dancing in a circle, a contagious, toothy grin plastered across his face.

At first, Russ tried to fight it, but then he broke into full-fledged laughter. His buddies soon followed, and before long, every guy was laughing, some with hands on knees, while the girls observed this confrontation of alpha males.

It turned out the guys from PA were a pretty decent lot. They were a few years older, and all had gone into the mines after high school. It was obvious that Russ still had a thing for Betty, who Johnny surmised had ended their relationship at some point, probably after Russ left school.

A couple of the guys from PA had been wrestlers in high school and hit it off with Brian, who was going to a small school in their state on a wrestling scholarship. It turned out they had participated in a tri-state tournament back when Brian was a sophomore. There was plenty of food to go around, and Russ had brought a huge cooler packed with ice-cold beer.

After they had eaten and that first blush of meeting someone new had worn off, it became evident that there were two guys for each girl. Russ, who turned out to be a gregarious, funny guy, seemed to realize that it was over with Betty, who had been friendly to him but reserved. But when Johnny talked, her expression was that of someone admiring an exquisite item that was out of her price range in a storefront window.

The other girls had also shown little interest in Russ's buddies. They seemed to look upon them as damaged goods, as something they were trying to get away from, a life in a small, rural town in coal country.

Russ and his buddies eventually departed but not before everyone shook hands. The two wrestlers wished Brian the best in wrestling in college. There was a *fait accompli* about them, as if their lives' journeys were already determined—forty years of hard and dangerous manual labor in a mine followed by respiratory problems if they lived long enough, their life expectancy probably not much longer than Johnny's.

Brian and Brad then took their girls for walks on the beach while the rest paired off in the backyard, except for Betty and Johnny. She grabbed his hand. "Come with me," she said in a detached yet possessive voice, her tight grip on his hand shooting a wild surge through Johnny as she led him to a bedroom with a queen-size bed taking up most of the space.

A light on the nightstand was on. Betty turned it off, plunging the room suddenly into dusky darkness. She sat on the bed, her face a shadow. "I know I'll never see you again," she said, looking up at Johnny.

He stood there, not sure what his next move should be, when she stood and brought herself close to him, her face in his, her hot breath enticing. "I want something to remember you by," she said. She tilted her head to the side, her eyes searching Johnny's. He kissed her, their bodies tight, arms wrapped around each other, her tongue probing deep into his mouth with a hunger Johnny had never before experienced.

They fell onto the bed, Johnny on top of her. He cupped her breast, and she did not resist. Soon they were naked, her strong body warm and exhilarating. "Don't come inside me," she whispered in a husky rasp as she began to bring him in to her.

Johnny pulled back as he thought of her possibly carrying his child, a child who could be missing the same critical gene. "No," he groaned. "I can't."

"What?" Betty said coldly in his ear.

"I don't want to take a chance on you getting pregnant."

"No problem." She slid out from under him and sat on the edge of the bed, rifling through her purse on the floor. Johnny watched, stretched out with elbow cocked, chin on palm, her back to him. The glow of moonlight creeping through the blinds slashed bars of light across her silky-skinned back, running parallel to the white streak from her bra strap. How enticing. She turned and said, "Let me do the honors," as she tore open a small plastic packet. A rubber emerged. "Oh," she said, wiggling Johnny's member, "you're still good to go."

Afterward, as they lay in bed facing each other, she ran her hand through his hair and said, "Do you know how beautiful you are?" Betty placed her hand on Johnny's cheek. "You've got it all: looks, charm, and smarts." She kissed him lightly on the lips and leaned back, her eyes appraising. "You're one of the lucky ones."

"Things aren't always what they appear to be," Johnny said.

"Those boys from Pennsylvania," she said in a changed voice, "would swap places with you in a heartbeat."

"You're very wise, aren't you?" Johnny said, his gaze deep into Betty's. "And you know what? I wouldn't change places with them, either, for all the heartbeats in the world."

CHAPTER 9

END OF THE WONDER YEARS

"You could get into any college you want, Johnny," Danny said. It was the tail end of summer, and the two boys were in the parking lot of Central Liquors, right across the DC line, sitting in the Gray Ghost.

Johnny took a sip of a quart bottle of beer and handed it back to Danny. "Money, Danny. My mother doesn't have a lot."

Danny took a long, thirsty swallow and let out an "Ahh, yeah, man." He looked at Johnny, a puzzled expression on his face. "Yeah, but MJC," he said as he peeled the Schlitz label off the bottle. "What about the football scholarship to Dickinson?"

Johnny took the bottle from Danny, started to drink, and stopped. "I couldn't leave my mother alone."

"She still having a tough time about your dad and all," Danny said, more as a statement than question. "I can't believe Maryland didn't give you a baseball scholarship. You were the best player in the county."

97

"Coach said they're loaded at my position, but I am welcome to try out."

"What bullshit," Danny said as he reached for the bottle from Johnny and took a long swallow, finishing it off.

"Wouldn't be the same, anyway," Johnny said as he turned on the motor to the Gray Ghost. "It would never be like what we had with the Bethesda Colts in junior high and at WJ."

"You talk to the coaches at MJC?"

No," Johnny said through a sigh. "I'm done with organized sports."

"Too rinky-dink?"

"No, not that, just wouldn't be the same, Danny."

Johnny was the only one of the boys who would attend Montgomery Junior College, or MJC, as it was called. Mickey was off to prep school for a year, Tip and Danny to Maryland, and Brad and Brian out of state on their athletic scholarships. Johnny felt like the captain of the Good Ship Ayrlawn, and all his mates were abandoning him.

"I wish we could start it all over again, Danny," Johnny said.

"Part of me does, but another part is glad to be moving on," Danny said as he stuffed the empty beer bottle under the seat. "I'm looking forward to the freedom of sharing a dorm room with Tip with no curfew and pledging SAE. Their parties are supposed to be great."

Johnny felt like saying, *You're moving on, and I'm stuck at home with my mother and a bad ticker to boot.* Instead, he said with a lift in his voice, "Let's live out our last days in the glow of high school and hit this party in Chevy Chase with all the pretty girls you've been telling me so much about."

"Sounds like a plan," Danny said, nodding. "A real good one."

* * *

98

MJC was where most of the kids who didn't have the money or grades to attend a four-year school went. The campus, if you could call it that, was in Takoma Park. The buildings were old brick structures, and it seemed more like an extension of high school than college.

Tip and Danny, on the other hand, were immersed in a brand-new social scene at Maryland: frat parties on Friday night at a local fire hall, football games at Byrd Stadium on Saturday afternoons, and more parties afterward. They invited Johnny to join them at a game or frat party, but he always declined. His life became routine: attend class during the day—he was taking twenty hours with a goal of graduating in three semesters—go home and study, maybe go down to Ayrlawn and shoot hoops by himself, dinner, more homework, a little TV, and lights out. He knew some of the kids at MJC, mostly athletes he had competed against over the years. They were good guys, and Johnny attended a few parties, but it wasn't the same.

One day after class, he was down at Ayrlawn shooting hoops by himself when he heard a familiar voice. "Johnny." He looked up to see Danny jogging up to him.

"Danny McKenzie, me boy, haven't seen you for a while."

Big boy Danny was still maturing, a late bloomer, and had been Johnny's best friend from the get-go. They had always been comfortable together, fair-haired Danny with his dimpled baby face and the shorter, leaner Johnny with his good looks and charisma.

"Just like the first time we met," Johnny said as he bounce-passed the ball to Danny. "Me and you with Ayrlawn all to ourselves."

"Except for the school, it's pretty much the same," Danny said, lifting his chin in the direction of the brick wall, beyond which stood Ayrlawn Elementary School, which had been built a few years back.

Danny tossed the ball back to Johnny, and he lined up a shot from the corner and fired away. The ball swished through the chained net—*cling*—bouncing back to Johnny as if on a string. "Do you remember that day?" he said, passing Danny the ball.

"Yeah, I was throwing a tennis ball against the wall."

"I called out to you, 'Hey, lefty, wanna play catch?'"

Danny nodded. "Yeah, I could tell right away you were a good ballplayer." He shot from beyond the foul line, and the ball clanged off the back of the rim onto the top of the backboard, bouncing wildly onto the grass.

Johnny hustled after it and returned to the court. He cradled the ball under his arm, scanning Ayrlawn—Moo Moo in all her green glory still whirling atop the silo, the patch of woods on a rise near the big backstop. Then his eyes settled on the field, the wide expanse of grass and patches of dirt. "We had some great times here, didn't we?" He looked at Danny, lost in the memories. "Best time ever was with the Colts and Mr. Harper. It was something else."

"I'll never forget the game against Rockville for the championship," Danny said. "You won the day, Johnny."

Johnny bounced passed the ball to Danny. "It was the best game ever."

"And the best part for me," Danny said as he dribbled the ball in front of himself, "was you shutting up that middle linebacker who was running his mouth all day." He tossed the ball back to Johnny.

"That was sweet," Johnny said. He remembered his best part as Mr. Harper picking him up in a big bear hug, his scent of Old Spice and tobacco so strong and reassuring, as were the big man's words: "You got heart, Johnny, a big heart, son."

Johnny turned toward the basket and shot, banking it in off the backboard through the net. "Play a game of HORSE?"

"Can't," Danny said. "I just stopped at home to pick up some clothes, and I have to get back for a pledge meeting at my frat house."

"How's that going?"

"It's pretty good," Danny replied. "Some of the older guys are assholes, but the parties are fun." A breeze picked up, putting a sudden chill in the air, and Danny looked up at the gray November sky. "Wish you'd come to one of the frat parties, Johnny."

"Nah," Johnny said as he bounced the ball once and then tucked it under his arm. "It's not for me."

Danny nodded as though understanding and said, "How's it going at MJC?"

Johnny twirled the ball on his ring finger. "It's okay," he said as he spun the ball with his free hand.

"Met any girls?"

Johnny lost control of the ball, and it bounced toward Danny, who caught it. "A few dates but nothing serious," Johnny said.

Danny tossed the ball to Johnny and said, "Bet you have a girlfriend by next semester."

*   *   *

Danny's prediction came true. During the first day of American Literature, Johnny found himself sitting next to Jeannie Hendrickson, a real looker—natural blond with a great figure, a beautiful take-home-to-Mom face, and twilight-blue eyes that radiated an inner warmth. She'd had a steady beau from Whitman, but he was away to college, and guys at MJC had been asking her out right and left. Johnny knew her in passing from a few parties in Potomac. Her beauty was similar to Betsy's, but her personality was quieter, not to the extent of Barbara, but somewhere in between his two former girlfriends.

Nothing happened between them at first, other than friendly banter about friends they shared. Then one day before class, Johnny asked her if she was going to the Sadie Hawkins dance in the school gym.

"You going, Johnny?"

"Haven't been asked yet." He smiled his killer smile. Soon, they were dating—drive-in movies and beers at the Zephyr, a cozy little bar on the second floor of a row house in northwest DC where a lot of the kids hung out. DC was the place to go since the drinking age was eighteen. Jeannie seemed a perfect girl for Johnny, not stuck up about her good looks and a lot of fun to be with.

They had sex on two occasions in the backseat of Johnny's car, once at a drive-in movie and the other in a secluded park. They were each other's second lover. Both times were a tumbledown affair of Johnny sliding his pants down and securing a rubber, and Jeannie slipping out of her undies and lifting her skirt. It was hot and steamy sex with Jeannie writhing and moaning, her arms clinging around Johnny's neck, her hot breath in his ear as she whispered, "I love you, Johnny, I love you." There was a trace of desperation in her tone as if she realized he didn't love her back. After, they silently slipped back into their clothes, Johnny a bit uneasy on both occasions as he realized that she had fallen hard for him.

Also, his condition was creeping more and more to the forefront of his mind. He would be limited for the rest of his life in his relationship with a woman. He could be dead at forty, maybe sooner. How could he get serious with any woman when he could die on her way too early? So he used his heart as his excuse to himself and broke it off with Jeannie, telling her that she was a great girl, and it wasn't her, but that he wasn't ready to get serious.

At first, Jeannie was crushed, but she soon recovered when, that summer, he saw her at a party in Potomac with her high school sweetheart all lovey-dovey. She ignored Johnny as if he were not there. It wasn't an icy rejection but more as though she hardly knew him. Johnny felt bad that he had put Jeannie in such an awkward spot. This romance business was tricky enough, he thought, but when you have a shortened life span due to a bad heart, it only complicated matters.

After three semesters of twenty hours each, Johnny graduated with an associate's degree. Academically, he had found MJC similar to WJ, except the kids weren't as smart. He read his assignments, showed up for class and took notes, and looked them over before an exam, no problem. But he had tired of school—and for that matter, his life. Ever since high school, he had felt detached, as though going through the motions. He remembered his promise to himself—*carpe diem*. He wasn't seizing the day; he was going through life on autopilot. He had his twentieth birthday coming up soon, and it struck him that he was halfway to forty.

Johnny considered getting a student loan to finish up a four-year degree, but he saw no purpose. What good would it do to bust his ass working at some nine-to-five job, only to have his career cut short by death? Plus, he didn't like the idea of working indoors, cramped in an office. He wanted something open and free like he had at Ayrlawn, with the change of seasons in the air and his body exerting itself.

When he told his mother he was finished with college for good, she tried to talk out of it at first, but finally he said, "Mom, what's the purpose of it?"

Mary O'Brien dropped her gaze and sighed. She looked up at Johnny and said with surrender in her voice, "It's your life. Live it as you see fit."

With the Vietnam War heating up and the draft calling anyone not in college for an Army physical, there was one silver lining with his condition: he was classified 4F.

He told Danny that he failed because of the heart murmur. "I thought it wasn't a problem," Danny said. They were in a booth at the Piccolo, a dive bar right over the DC line on Connecticut Avenue.

Johnny looked out the window at the sun sinking below the dusky horizon, pedestrians bustling along the sidewalk, wrapped in scarves and heavy coats against the windy cold of early March. "It's not, really," Johnny said, as he turned back toward his friend. "But," he said with a shrug, "they didn't want me."

There was a question in Danny's eyes: *You hiding something, Johnny?* But that's as far as Danny would go. If his best friend wanted to keep a secret, then so be it.

After MJC, Johnny got a job working for a former neighbor who was a builder. Johnny began as a laborer on a four-story office building going up in Rockville. Within a couple of weeks on the job, he was promoted to carpenter's assistant, and soon he was a jack of all trades. During Christmas break from school that year, Danny needed some spending money for the spring term, and Johnny got him a temp job working alongside him.

Johnny worked hard and smart, his sharp eyes missing nothing. "Hey, pisano," he said to a carpenter whom he and Danny were bringing two-by-sixes to, "those studs are supposed to be sixteen inches apart, not eighteen."

The carpenter, an older Italian fellow, lowered his hammer and stood back from a line of studs he had nailed to a toeplate. He looked over his shoulder and said, "Thanks, Johnny. Boss man, he would no like that."

Later that day, when Johnny and Danny were stripping stringers from the bottom of a concrete floor that had recently been poured, Johnny noticed large pockmarks in the concrete. "Look at those honeycombs," he said, shaking his head. "They didn't oil those stringers properly." Without checking with anyone, he got a bag of portland cement from the supply shed and showed Danny how to mix and grout a patch job on a concrete surface—upside down, no less. "Not too much water, Danny," he said as Danny poured water from a bucket into a wheelbarrow of cement while Johnny stood on a ladder with a mortar board and trowel.

Johnny had free reign on the job. He and Danny pitched in where needed, with Johnny talking construction lingo as if he were an old hand. "Ah, another day of sleever bars and bull pins," he shouted to an ironworker.

"Johnny," the man said, "can you guys give me a hand later today cutting rebar?"

"Thought you'd never ask," Johnny said, never stopping as he and Danny hauled the stringers they had scraped clean and oiled to the edge of the third floor for the crane.

It felt great having Danny with him all day, his best friend working at his side and picking things up quickly. By the end of Danny's first week, they were a competent team. A couple times after work, they went out for beers, shooting the breeze about girls and sports, and Johnny felt almost like his old self again.

But after two weeks, Danny returned to the U of Maryland and the frat life of keg parties. At first, Johnny missed his friend's companionship, but soon he immersed himself in his job, trying to learn all that he could about the construction industry. He had established himself as not only well liked but respected by this hard-nut crew of thirty or so construction workers, of which Johnny knew every name. He helped carpenters frame, hung drywall, set stringers, cut rebar, and cleaned and swept up where needed. Johnny even made a suggestion to the foreman about using a different type of oil on the stringers, which resulted in fewer honeycombs.

During that time, Johnny's mother ran into the builder at the grocery store. He told her that Johnny was a wonderful worker—"so very bright and likable." She told Johnny that the builder had told her, "Your son would make a very fine architect. It's as though he has a set of blueprints in his mind."

But after two and a half years, Johnny quit the construction business. Though he enjoyed outdoor work, he tired of the mach-speed pace and constant drone of heavy equipment.

Here he was, while his friends were out into the world on their own, still living with his mother. He would have loved to have moved into the apartment that Tip and Danny rented, but he couldn't leave his mother alone. She had never recovered from the death of her husband. Her life still revolved around her son, her work, and her house.

Johnny would never forget the day they moved into the house, his mother's eyes glittering happiness, that knowing look spreading across her face as though her dream had finally come true. Mary O'Brien's house and her family sustained her, were her reason for existing. She had experienced a few months of bliss, where each morning after feeding her husband and son breakfast, she got dressed and went over to a neighbor's kitchen for an hour of gossip and cigarettes with her new girlfriends. Then she returned to her very own house to clean and prepare dinner for her family.

And then that terrible day, when her glowing aura had been replaced by a shell-shocked expression. A different spirit had entered her being, a sad, broken-hearted spirit. Johnny could never leave her all alone.

After the construction job, Johnny tended bar at Hennessey's Tavern on Wisconsin Avenue in Bethesda, which was frequented by people his mother's age and older. He was a big hit, talking sports with the regulars and charming all the ladies. But by age twenty-six, when most of his friends had embarked on professional careers, Johnny had tired of working for someone else. He wanted to be the hero in his own life, to steer his own course without anyone else at the helm.

"I got an idea," he told Danny as his friend came into Hennessey's one day after work.

"Uh-huh," Danny said as he loosened his tie. "Pour me a cold one first."

"Sure thing," Johnny said as he tapped a draft beer and handed it to his friend. "Another day at the salt mines?"

Danny nodded and let out a stream of air between his lips. "Yeah," he said as he looked over Johnny's shoulder at knickknacks of toy racing cars and shot glasses on a shelf above the mirror. "Between night school for my CPA and working for that accounting firm . . . anyhow, what's your idea, Johnny?"

Johnny placed his hands on the counter and said in a low voice, "What if I told you I am going to start my own landscape company?"

Danny nearly gagged on his beer. "What? You don't know anything about that business."

Johnny brought his finger to his lips. "Not so loud." He told Danny that he had applied for a job working for a landscape company. "After they hire me—"

"Wait a minute," Danny interrupted. "What makes you think they're going to hire you?"

Johnny leaned back and straightened himself, his eyes smiling at Danny, when an order rang out from a group of local businessmen sitting at the corner of the bar.

Johnny went over and made up their drinks in rapid-fire order. His clever hands worked in unison to pour gin and vermouth in a mixing glass and shake the concoction in one hand while the other began working on a rum and Coke. All the while, Johnny told one of his many jokes to the men, who erupted in laughter. "Johnny, you and your stories," one man hooted. "You could go on stage."

He returned to Danny and topped off his beer. "On the house, Danny boy."

"Now, what makes you think you're going to get this landscape job?" Danny said as Johnny placed the mug in front of him.

"Danny, who can resist hiring me?"

Of course, Johnny was right. No one could resist him. He worked for the landscape company for one year through all four seasons, and when he told his boss he was going to quit, the man offered him a big raise and partial ownership down the road. But Johnny turned him down flat. Even if they did give him partial ownership, he would still be answering to someone else. He wanted freedom.

So Johnny started O'Brien Landscaping, purchasing an old bread truck for next to nothing. But he bought all his tools new. Among them were a posthole digger, short-handled spade, rounded and flat-end shovels, hatchet, axe, hedge clippers, bow saw, wrenches, and a contractor's wheelbarrow. All the truck had to do was get him to the job, but his tools needed to be sharp and strong. He had seen firsthand with his old company how poor tools or the wrong tool could adversely affect a job.

Johnny also printed up and distributed flyers around the Ayrlawn neighborhood and even went door to door, introducing himself and, on the spot, drawing up new designs for people's yards on eight-by-eleven white paper with circles, rectangles, and triangles weaving in intricate patterns representing bushes, trees, retaining walls, and even a detailed legend in the right-hand corner. It was work done by skilled hands, Johnny's hands, which seemed to have no limit for creativity.

Danny once asked him, "How did you do learn to draw landscape designs?"

"Eh," Johnny said as if it were no big deal, "books from the library."

Thanks to his popularity with the parents of his friends and neighbors around Ayrlawn, word spread throughout the neighborhood that Johnny O'Brien did good work for a reasonable price, and more than one woman told his mother that he was as charming as he was good-looking. No doubt, Johnny could have expanded the business into a booming success, but he worked by himself, keeping it simple. Why start up a business with employees depending on him when in less than twenty years he could drop dead at any time? So he mowed, mulched, planted new shrubs and trees, and shoveled walkways and driveways in the winter. After a big snow, Johnny would enter McDonald's Raw Bar with a fistful of bills, buying drinks all around, including the old boys at the bar.

The Raw Bar was in the heart of downtown Bethesda on Old Georgetown Road and a great place to hang out. The front room had tables and booths, in the middle was the bar where the old-timers hung out, and the back room was anchored by a big round table in the middle. Johnny had tried to get the boys to show up on Fridays after work, but attendance was spotty at best. He needed something to draw them out that they couldn't resist.

His solution was to rent the gym at Bethesda Elementary School on Fridays from five to seven. At first, it was only two-on-two basketball with Danny, Mickey, Tip, and Johnny. But soon Brad and Brian showed up, then a couple of the janitors at the school joined, and then some more guys trickled in until they had a full court game with a couple of subs rotating in. It soon became a must to show up and play and then afterwards to adjourn to the Raw Bar right around the corner from the gym. Life had not been this good since high school. It was one great place after another: Friday Night Basketball, as it came to be known, a refuge where everyone could forget their problems for a few hours and revert back to who they were in high school.

Ever since WJ, Johnny had missed the camaraderie of competitive sports with the boys. A flag football game at Ayrlawn over Thanksgiving just didn't do it. Friday Night Basketball seemed to reinvigorate him. These were hard-ass competitive games with banging, hard picks, and foul language galore. Johnny rarely swore and never argued, and when tempers rose and the potential for a fight erupted, he would get between the combatants and settle things down.

One time, Brad and Mickey got into it until they were standing toe to toe. They would have never come to blows, but an outsider would not have known it. "That was a whining, cheap-ass call, Doyle," Harper brayed.

"You elbow me in the chest and bull moose me out of the way for a layup?" Mickey was right in Brad's grille, spittle forming in little bubbles on his lips.

Brad sneered, "Start pushing some iron, Doyle, and quit crying." Harper had a good forty pounds on Mickey and used his bulk and strength to his advantage at all times on the court.

"Pushing iron?" Mickey's eyes seemed prepared to launch into orbit. "You are such the asshole, Harper."

"Enough, guys," Johnny said as he stepped in between them and turned to Brad. "Son, I say, *suuun*, is this any way to handle yourself on the court?" He turned and faced Mickey. "*Suuun?* We only have the gym for two hours."

A crack of a smile formed in the corner of Mickey's mouth, but there was still fire in his eyes, a competitive fire that infected everyone at Friday Night Basketball. "Fine, as long as I get my foul call."

Johnny turned to Brad. "You fouled him, Brad. Now, let's play."

"All right, fine. I fouled the pussy," Brad sneered at Mickey. "Why don't you wear a dress next week, Doyle?"

And so it went. Friday Night B-ball was a prime example of saying and doing things to friends that were never done in public—swearing a blue streak, Danny calling Brad a lying cheating blankety-blank, him giving it right back. After two hours of running and straining with everything they had, pent-up aggression depleted after a long work week, the boys headed over to the back room of McDonald's Raw Bar, where they hooted and laughed about whatever transgressions they had committed on each other—and there were plenty—while playing Liar's Poker over pitchers of beer and pizza. The back room had light-pine paneling, scuffed linoleum floors, and a ship wheel's clock on the wall offering a bit of a nautical flair. It was a worn, comfortable space where everybody knew your name.

CHAPTER 10

THE LOVE OF JOHNNY'S LIFE

The first year of Friday Night Basketball, a new waitress was hired at the Raw Bar. She sauntered right up to the round table and said, "So this must the boys of Bethesda I've heard so much about." She had lush brown eyes flecked with tiny bits of amber like stardust, eyes that took the boys in with a mischievous grin, stirring every guy at the table, including Johnny.

"That'd be us," Johnny replied as their eyes met. There was something in her stance, with the back of her hand on Mickey's chair, those devastating eyes holding Johnny's gaze, that said this girl was different. She wore her chestnut hair in a ponytail, and her body had curves and fat in all the right places to give shape to her shapeless white T-shirt. This was a good-looking, sexy girl.

"What's your name?" asked Mickey.

"Maggie. What's yours, Slim?"

This cracked up the table. "Hah, hah, Slim," Brad bellowed. "You're okay, honey." He then began introducing each of the boys to this new girl, who was perfectly at ease with a table of eight—some rather large and intimidating—men. Brad flicked his finger toward to the last guy. "This is Johnny."

"Hello, Johnny. You look like a cold beer kinda guy."

Johnny nodded, his eyes taking in the girl before him. "Looks like you got me figured out, Maggie."

It was a typical Friday night at the Raw Bar with talk at the table about the previous games, pizza, and Liar's Poker. That was all standard, as were the hootin' and hollerin' and laughing and arguing about nothing of any consequence, just a group of guys blowing off steam and kidding each other, such as Danny needling the rest of the table how Tip, Johnny, and he were the last bachelors. "We're still free men, without a curfew."

Just then, Maggie came up to clear away some empties amongst the din. "Mr. Freeman," she said to Danny with tongue firmly planted in cheek, "another pitcher for you and your shackled comrades?" While the table broke up in a roar of laughter, Johnny exchanged a look with Maggie and something passed between them—something he had never felt before.

By last call, Johnny and Danny were all that remained in the back room. The check had been paid, and they sat with a half-full pitcher of beer. Maggie had finished wiping down the tables, and Johnny asked her to join them.

She came over with an empty mug, poured herself a beer, and raised it to Johnny. "Ever had a chilly?" Her full, sensuous lips split into a take-your-breath-away smile, and in her gaze there was a ken of utter confidence, as if she had known him for years.

Johnny clinked her glass. Danny began to raise his but seemed to realize they barely even knew he was there at that point.

"Tell me about yourself, Maggie," Johnny said.

Maggie Meyers was from Northern California and had recently graduated from Maryland with a degree in English lit.

"You sticking around?" Johnny asked.

Maggie shrugged and took a drink of beer. She shrugged again and said, "Depends."

Danny soon departed, and it was just the two of them. They chatted amiably for a while, and then Johnny reached over and placed his hand on top of hers. "You're different."

Maggie flashed a smile at Johnny. "Your hand is like rawhide." She took his hand in hers and ran her fingers in a circle on his palm.

"Work."

"Ah," Maggie said as she stared at Johnny's palm. "Let me guess—carpenter."

"Landscaper."

Maggie continued to study Johnny's hand and then traced her index finger along a vertical line. "This is your fate line." She ran her finger along the line until it intersected a horizontal line toward the top of his hand. "It intersects your heart line."

"They're intertwined," Johnny said in a factual tone. He caught himself and said, "Are you a palm reader?"

"No," Maggie said. She looked at Johnny, her lovely brown eyes alert, her lips pursed as though she had discovered something. "My great aunt had some gypsy blood." Her eyes crinkled in self-depreciating delight. "We all have our secrets."

Johnny laced his fingers through hers and said, "You really are different, aren't you?"

Johnny and Maggie were soon a couple, and in this relationship, she was his equal in every way, never appearing overwhelmed by his looks and charisma. She laughed as hard as any of the boys at his jokes, and there was a glimmer in her eyes when she looked at him, but with it was a glint of determination. This girl had backbone. This girl was Johnny's equal in not only looks but whatever that magical, magnetic aura was that drew people to them.

At parties, the boys would often huddle in a corner while the wives conversed in the kitchen or living room about babies and home life. Maggie was equally adept at conversing with either group. She would stand in the kitchen and listen attentively about problems with babysitting or school and add cogent comments about her sister's kids back in California. "Oh, Janet, I wish my sister were here. She has the exact same problem with her son's nursery school teacher." Soon she was one of them, a single girl who was at ease with wives and girlfriends of the boys.

And she could just as easily slide into the guys' conversation about any sport under the sun, especially baseball. Danny found this out much to his chagrin at a party at Brad's house. "Book"—Mickey said the designation with a twist as if he had a good one for Danny—"who is the only player to drive in over one hundred runs his first eleven years in the big leagues?" Mickey, who had lost many an argument with Danny over baseball trivia, had anointed him "The Book."

Right about this time, Maggie came up next to Johnny and said, "Bet I know the answer." Mickey's eyes lit up like when he was a kid and had hit a winning basket at Ayrlawn.

"Don't say anything, Maggie. We have Mr. Book here, Mr. Know-It-All." Mickey swept his hands out toward Danny. He was really enjoying this, for Danny had a look of uncertainty.

"All right," Danny said, "let's see. It hasn't happened in at least the last twenty years . . . I figure it must have occurred during the thirties when there were big numbers in baseball."

"Book, would you like Maggie to give it a shot?" Mickey had the biggest shit-eating grin on his face.

Johnny also was enjoying his girlfriend's moment. "I do believe we may well have a new Book in our midst."

"Okay," Danny said, "it has gotta be Mel Ott."

"Wrong!" Mickey said. He turned to Maggie. "What do you say, my dear?"

Maggie raised her eyebrow toward Danny like a card player holding a straight flush. "Al Simmons," she said through a sly, little smile.

"Looks like we do have a new Book in town," Mickey crowed. He lifted Maggie's hand over her head. "You've got a winner here, Johnny."

Johnny wrapped his arm around Maggie's shoulder and said, "This girl never ceases to amaze me." He looked at her and said, "How did you know that?"

"My dad wanted a boy, and he got me instead," she said with a twinkle in her eye. "He used to play catch with me and talk baseball."

"Really?" Johnny said as he felt a twinge of envy.

"Oh, yeah," Maggie said with a shrug. "I was a tomboy."

"You sure don't look like a tomboy now," Mickey said with raised eyebrows and a naughty-boy smile.

Maggie was like Johnny in so many ways besides the personality and looks. She continued to work as a waitress at the Raw Bar when she no doubt could have found a career job. But she had that same free-spirited streak that Johnny had. They were both perfectly content with how they made their living, and Maggie seemed to enjoy every moment of waitressing. She loved Friday nights waiting on the boys and laughing right along.

Maggie also got to know Tip and Danny, who would frequent the Raw Bar with Johnny on Saturday afternoons after he got off work. The pace was slower at this time of day, and she often would sit with them and chitchat. She loved to read fiction and was an Agatha Christie fan, having read and reread all of her detective novels. She once told them, "There's something very enjoyable about cuddling on my sofa under an afghan on a rainy day and letting myself be swept away by a good whodunit. You never know how it's going to end." She leaned back in her chair, scanned the nearly empty back room, and turned her gaze back to the table. "Sort of like life," she said.

Six months into the relationship, Johnny had fallen head-over-heels for this intriguing girl. He hadn't told her anything about his heart condition, though when she had read his palm that first night, he suspected she was onto something. Though he would not marry and would definitely not want to pass his genes on to another life, he could not imagine not having her in his life. But it wasn't fair to Maggie to marry her and then die on her. He may well have had less than twenty years left; there was no telling. It was a real dilemma.

Though Johnny had not seen a doctor since Dr. Fitzgerald retired, he had gone to the medical library at the National Institutes of Health in Bethesda and researched his heart condition. The only advance in medicine that would pertain to him was a heart transplant. But most of the patients died within months of the operation due to the body's natural tendency to reject the new tissue—some option. Possibly down the road, the surgery would be more successful, but he could not imagine having his heart ripped from his chest and a stranger's heart put in its place. No, Johnny thought, he would stick with the one he was born with. And of course, the strange part of it was, he felt great.

Maggie had made no advances regarding marriage, but he sensed that if he asked, she would say yes. He had never gotten this far in a relationship, partly because he had never felt about anyone the way he did Maggie. But there was also that relentless little voice that was always reminding him of his uncertain future. He realized he needed to tell her soon.

Matters came to a head on a Saturday night at Maggie's apartment. Her roommate was out of town for the weekend. Maggie was going to cook Johnny dinner, and then maybe they would go out to a movie.

When Johnny arrived at the apartment, the aroma of spaghetti and meatballs greeted him when she answered the door with a frosted mug in hand. "Smells great in here," Johnny said as he kissed her on the cheek.

Maggie handed Johnny the mug of beer. "Ever had a chilly?" she said through her beguiling smile.

They sat on a comfortable, squishy sofa in the living room, Maggie sipping on wine and Johnny his beer. The space was decorated with offset shelves of odds and ends such as a cottage clock, a miniature lantern, and a metal vase with daisies. In a corner was a three-tier wire storage stand, each shelf containing a bird's nest with a colorful songbird nesting. Johnny always felt at ease in this cozy, warm setting.

He looked out the patio sliding glass door, the spring weather outside wet, cold, and blustery. "This rain is putting me behind schedule," he said with a shake of his head. "No matter. How are you feeling, my lovely?" They had not seen each other for nearly a week, Johnny being busy with work and Maggie having just recovered from the flu.

"I'm not contagious anymore," Maggie said as she placed her hand on Johnny's cheek.

Johnny leaned in and kissed her. Her honeysuckle scent, her touch, and the warmth of her body and spirit filled him with sensual delight.

Maggie stood and took Johnny's hand. "Come with me, Johnny O'Brien, and I'll let you have your way with me."

Johnny hopped right up and said, "Maggie Meyers, you do have a way about you."

Later that evening, while Johnny helped Maggie with the dishes, he thought about their lovemaking earlier in the evening. It had been tender yet raunchy, a pleasurable combination of lust and love, a new type of happiness that was different from his joy at Ayrlawn as a boy, something more intricate and complex—two people giving of themselves to each other. He couldn't wait any longer, no matter what came of it. He had to tell her. She deserved the truth.

As Johnny dried the last dish, Maggie folded her apron and put it in a drawer.

"Can we talk?" Johnny heard the seriousness in his voice.

Maggie turned to Johnny with a look of frank appraisal. "Let's sit down in the living room."

They sat back on the sofa as the room seemed to swell with tension. Johnny breathed out and collected himself. He took Maggie's hand in his. "I have a heart condition." He looked at her, her eyes saying, *Go on.* "My father died of it at forty-two, and it can hit me most likely anytime after forty." He shrugged and said, "Maybe sooner."

"Oh, Johnny," Maggie said as she leaned her head on his shoulder.

"Also," Johnny said in a defeated voice, "I can pass it on to my progeny."

"If you ask me, I will say yes."

"I know you would, Maggie, but I cannot do it to you."

Maggie looked at Johnny, her eyes searching his face. "I would consider adoption."

There were so many things Johnny wanted to say to her at that moment, but instead, he shook his head. "No, Maggie, I am never going to marry." A pause settled between them, and then Johnny said, "Life is so damn unfair."

The next morning, Johnny and Maggie arose early and dressed in silence. Outside her bedroom window, the wind rattled against the pane. Johnny looked out at the gloomy, gray day. Part of him wanted to tell her that he would marry and have children and go anywhere she wanted on this earth. But that little voice was front and center and kept whispering, *Do you want to leave Maggie with no husband and a fatherless child with a ticking time bomb of a heart? Look what it did to your mother. Maggie deserves a better life.*

Johnny was sitting on the edge of the bed as Maggie slipped a sweater on. "Maggie—"

"I have thought about it," Maggie interrupted as she sat on the bed next to Johnny. She placed her hand on his cheek and held it there. "I respect your decision, Johnny."

Johnny reached for her hand on his cheek and kissed it. "I hoped you would," he said as he held her gaze in his, and in it saw what was coming next.

"I will be returning to California in the next couple of days." She leaned toward him and kissed him so very softly on the lips. "I will always have a place in my heart for you, Johnny—always."

*   *   *

Johnny didn't work or leave his bedroom for the next three days other than to use the bathroom and sip on some soup his mother made for him. He had told her he wasn't feeling well, but he saw in her gaze that she realized it had something to do with his heart condition and Maggie. Mary O'Brien had met Maggie a couple of times and told Johnny how fond she was of her. "A lovely girl," she had said more than once, "and so very practical and down to earth."

By the end of the week, Johnny had returned to work—digging postholes for a new fence, mixing bags of concrete, mowing, trimming, and mulching as he traveled from job to job, losing himself in the endless work. He skipped Friday Night Basketball without even a call to Danny to give him a heads up.

The following week, Johnny was trimming bushes at a neighbor's house when he heard the patter of approaching footsteps. He turned to find Danny dressed in a business suit, squinting as though trying to find the right words. Johnny imagined how he must have looked to his good friend—the usual vibration of energy deadened, sleep-deprived eyes streaked red, slump-shouldered stance of defeat.

Johnny stood there staring at Danny, who finally said, "We heard about Maggie leaving town at the Raw Bar last Friday."

Johnny turned back to the bushes and began trimming.

Danny reached for Johnny's wrist to stop him, but he jerked away, continuing to work. "Johnny, stop for a second and sit down and talk to me."

Johnny lowered the clippers to his side and said over his shoulder, "Danny, from the first time we met, I knew you'd be a friend of mine." Johnny turned and faced him. "It turns out," he said in a voice trying to rally his spirits, "you became my best friend." He drew a breath and cleared his throat. "There isn't anything I would not do for you. But I will not talk about what happened with Maggie." He looked hard at Danny. "It's in the past, she's in the past—she's a memory—a very fine memory."

* * *

Johnny didn't see his friends for a couple more weeks before showing back up at the Raw Bar after Friday Night Basketball. "Johnny!" the boys shouted as he shuffled over to the round table in his easy gait.

Johnny raised his fist toward the bar, then raised and lowered his thumb for a draft as if he'd had never been gone. He surveyed the back room. Everything looked the same: the ship wheel's clock hanging on the wall, two-man and four-man tables lining the perimeter, the pine paneling seeming to shine with a glow as if welcoming Johnny back. "Boys," he said as he sat between Danny and Tip.

"You over Maggie?" Brian said, tucking his chin into his thick neck as though retreating from a quick attack. Johnny's expression was blank save for his normally placid eyes, now a pair of hard dark things.

"Shut up," Danny said from across the table. "What gets into you sometimes, Brian?"

An uneasy silence fell over the table before Johnny said, "It's okay, Danny." But it was not okay. Brian's comment stung to the core, but Johnny was determined not to show it.

The waitress came over, served Johnny his beer, and then took orders from the rest of the table. Danny, still staring daggers at Brian, ordered a pitcher. Mickey and Tip ordered bottled beers. Brad and Brian were good.

"So what have I have I missed at b-ball?" Johnny asked.

"Not the same without you," Brian said in a conciliatory tone. "Doyle and Harper arguing wasted a good fifteen minutes."

Over a few beers, the games were rehashed, and it was good medicine for Johnny to be in the company of his best friends and drink a beer or two—which he hadn't had in over three weeks—relaxing his mind and body.

After the games had been thoroughly analyzed and bickered over with good-humored ribbing, Danny said, "What's old Scruffy Lomax been up to?" Scruffy was a fictional character of Johnny's, who over the last couple of years he had told outrageous yarns about him. Besides Scruffy Lomax, he had developed an ensemble of characters, all trappers, gamblers, and prospectors from a made-up place called Big Bear, Alaska: Needle Nose Latrobe, Pistol Pete Pidantes, Frenchy Dupree, and Scruffy's one-eyed mongrel, Rusty the One-Eyed Wonder Dog.

"I got a good story for you guys," Johnny said. "Let me conjure ol' Scruffy up." He lowered his head as though praying and said, "Scruffy, you in there? . . . I'm here, pardner," Johnny said out of the side of his mouth with an earthy twang like an old-timer in a '50s western. "Let me out and say hi to the boys." Johnny looked around the table, his buddies all smiling big with anticipation.

"You promise to behave?" Johnny said in his regular voice.

"Promise," Scruffy growled.

"Alrighty, then."

Johnny then squeezed his shoulders in, drew his chin into his neck, and said in his gravelly Scruffy voice, "Pardners, so good to be back in your company—ha ha ha."

"We need a story, Scruffy," Brad said in a loud, demanding voice as he pounded his big fist on the table, rattling the mugs and drawing the attention of nearby tables.

"Well, since I last saw you fellers," Scruffy said, "Rusty and I got captured and escaped from a pack of Bigfoot."

Johnny was in character. He was Scruffy Lomax. At a nearby table, a young couple was listening with rapt attention as though believing every word like children hearing a bedtime story. Johnny told how Frenchy Dupree and Scruffy had been prospecting out on the tundra, when a blizzard hit. "I grabbed Rusty under me arm and hunkered down upwind against a big rock, but the snowy wind and cold were something fierce." Johnny scratched his chin like a card shark holding four aces. "I blacked out, and next I know, me and Rusty are in a giant lair constructed of tree branches, like a wooden teepee. Smelled somethin' fierce—worse than any skunk you ever smelt. Didn't know what happened to Frenchy.

"Then I hear some rustlin', and in comes the biggest damn creature I ever did see. It was a Sasquatch, nine foot tall, followed by two smaller ones. Must have been the missus and daughter. Both had tits, so help me. The ones on Mommy would've stopped a team of oxen dead in their tracks." Not only the round table but tables nearby broke up in hooting, mug-clattering laughter.

Johnny then stood and raised his hands to silence his audience, for he now had the attention of the entire back room. He then closed one eye and opened the other wide, his face twisted in gnarly delight. "The only thing that saved me was me little red dog, Rusty, the One-Eyed Wonder Dog." Johnny paused for a moment and looked around the room. No one was moving. The waitress was hovering nearby, lost in the story. "I picked up Rusty so the evil eye pointed at that big ol' smelly thing, and me old red dog gave him the grin." Johnny offered a sideways grin—the corner of his mouth slashing across his cheek, revealing a row of bicuspids and molars. He did a 360, so everyone got a good look. "Well you'd a-thunk that big old ape had seen his maker. He let out a shriek damn near deafened me. I then sashayed out of the hut, nice and easy-like, holding Rusty close."

Johnny went on to tell of Scruffy's difficult journey getting back to the Lone Wolf Saloon, Rusty dying on him, then thawing back to life atop the bar at the Lone Wolf, and then a vengeful Frenchy showing up enraged at Scruffy for deserting him. But Rusty gave Frenchy the evil eye, and he froze in his tracks. Scruffy told Frenchy and a packed bar of trappers and prospectors his Bigfoot adventure, and all was well once again in Big Bear, Alaska. Johnny finished the story by raising his hand as if taking an oath. "I, Scruffy Lomax, and me little red dog live to fight another day."

Johnny then bowed with hand across waist and said in his normal voice, "That is the entertainment for the evening, folks."

The boys began to applaud, Brian exclaiming, "Scruffy's the man." The rest of the room then started clapping, and one fellow even let out a shrieking whistle. Johnny raised his hands, said thank you, and sat down. He looked around the table and said, "Ol' Scruffy does take a toll on a body."

The experience had a cathartic effect on Johnny. During the telling of his tale, he felt his energy surge and his spirit return, reinforcing the welcoming sense that it was good to be back amongst his friends and in a comfortable, familiar place like the Raw Bar.

However, beneath the bonhomie and spiritual healing, Johnny felt a hard edge about himself, sort of like the girls from Pennsylvania during senior week at the beach. Life had plastered him but good with Maggie's departure, and to combat it, Johnny had sunk his energies into work, trying to forget the pain of letting her go. During the spring and summer months, he worked sunrise to sunset six days a week, save for Friday Night Basketball. Tired after a week of digging, planting, mulching, and mowing, Johnny completely drained himself playing ball.

*   *   *

By the following spring, Johnny had tried to bury the loss of Maggie in a little compartment next to the one holding the root of all his problems—his heart condition—but she was never far from his thoughts. He dated sporadically but never allowed things to get serious, always comparing the girl to Maggie.

Johnny would meet Danny and/or Tip down at the Raw Bar for a couple of beers during the week, but he mostly spent evenings at home with his mother, working his way through the collection of Agatha Christie novels that Maggie had been such a fan of. He enjoyed these whodunits and would catch himself thinking of Maggie cuddled up on her sofa, lost in the world of Hercule Poirot. He checked out some of the books from the library, and he scoured bookstores for what they didn't have. By the year's end, he had read all but one. He saved *Murder on the Orient Express* for last and thoroughly enjoyed how the author made such an improbable tale so real. When he had finished, he felt a sense of release, as though he had completed a task that he had enjoyed but was now time to move on from. He donated the books to Goodwill and tucked away his time spent with Maggie as a cherished memory he could live with.

CHAPTER 11

A BACHELOR'S LIFE

It was a Saturday afternoon in early June, and Johnny was putting the finishing touches on a flower bed he had planted around a lilac bush. It was his thirtieth year, and his life had reached a comfortable yet predictable pattern: work long days from spring through autumn and taper off in winter. As he spread the mulch with his hands amongst the crocus, he thought about the last few years and the change that had come over his mother—which he was responsible for.

In the past, he had tried to ease her burden by volunteering to help with the cooking—though at the time, he had minimal skills— but she would have none of it. "I wouldn't think of it, Johnny, after you've worked so hard all day." She would whisk her hand at him to shoo him from her kitchen. But he grew determined to help his mother out and devised a strategy that began with talking to her about his paying to have a maid clean the house on a weekly basis.

"I am not having a stranger clean my house."

"But," Johnny replied, "wouldn't it be nice to not have to clean and do laundry on Saturdays?" They were eating dinner, and Johnny reached across the table and put his hand on his mother's forearm. "To be able to take your time in the kitchen while listening to your gardening show on the weekend instead of cleaning the house all day?"

Mary drew back from her son, her eyes saying yes but her lips set in tight denial. "I don't—"

Johnny cut in. "I've already hired her. She works for Mrs. McKenzie." It was a bit of a fib. He had only talked with the cleaning lady. "Danny says she's really nice and does a great job for his mom."

"Oh," Mary said, nodding as the idea of Saturdays to herself in her kitchen seemed to take hold. And so it began that Mary spent her Saturday piddling in the kitchen, part of her old life returning, before she returned to work on Monday.

After that, Johnny waited for the right moment, and one day when he and his mother were in the garden in the back yard, he said, "I would like to pay you rent, Mom."

A look came over Mary as if she had never heard of anything so preposterous. "My son shall never pay rent in my house."

"Mom," Johnny replied, stretching the word out, *Mommm*, as he tore open a bag of compost and began to mix it into the soil with a hoe. "I am not going to argue with you. You are going to take my money." He straightened himself and turned to Mary, who stood at the garden's edge with a look of dismayed pride—pride in her son and dismay that he would pay her rent.

Mary O'Brien was beginning to not only accept the fact that she didn't have to do it all but that she could rely on her son and not feel guilty about it. Though she didn't have that happy glow about her as when her husband was alive, Mary now spent time in her kitchen on the weekend listening to the radio and smoking a cigarette or two while she prepared meals at a slow and pleasurable pace.

As Johnny swept bits of loose mulch off the brick border of the lilac bush, he thought about how his mother had reached a level of contentment with her life. She still was not close to her old self, but there was a quiet certitude, a confidence that she wasn't in it alone, that her son was there for her. In the middle of dinner one evening recently, Mary had cut into her meat loaf with a fork and stopped. She looked over at her son and said, "You've taken a great load off my shoulders, Johnny."

Johnny looked up at his mother. "I should have done it earlier, Mom."

"No," Mary said, shaking her head, "I wasn't ready, nor were you."

It struck Johnny as he placed the extra crocus in a cardboard box on the passenger seat of his van that he had turned a corner in his life, a sharp corner. He had made some adult decisions about what was best for his mother and had stuck to his guns when she tried to resist.

When he got home from work Johnny found a note on the dining room table that his mother was out shopping. A warm, familiar aroma drew Johnny into the kitchen, where he lifted the lid of the cast iron pot and pinched a bite of his mother's pot roast.

At the sound of a car door slamming shut, he peeked out the window, expecting his mother, and saw a Montgomery County police cruiser parked on the street and the officer heading toward the house. Johnny opened the front door. Panic swarmed in his chest as he saw the pained expression on the officer's face. After identifying himself as Mary O'Brien's son, Johnny said, "Is she all right?"

The officer looked down for a moment and then faced Johnny. "I'm afraid she was hit by a truck crossing Wisconsin Avenue." He took a breath and said with a tone of finality, "Your mother didn't make it."

After the officer left, Johnny sat on the sofa and wept. Never in his life had he cried like this, big gobs of tears streaking his cheeks. Never in his life had he felt such numbing pain—not when his father died, nor when he got his heart diagnosis, not even when Maggie left him. This one hit him in a low, gut-level spot that he never knew existed. Johnny wiped the last of the tears off his face and drew a deep breath. He could almost feel his mother's hand on the back of his neck and her soft voice whispering in his ear, "It will be okay, honey. It will be okay."

Mary O'Brien had always been there to nurture her son, and after his father's death even more so. Her little boy had been the most important person in her life, her only child, whom she fussed over and tried to protect from the harsh realties of life, her little boy Johnny with a bad ticker whom she had prevented from playing football that first year of Bethesda Colts. How she had worried at home alone each game day, even more so during high school, too afraid to go watch her boy play "such a violent game." But she was always there with a steaming bowl of soup and sandwiches when he returned home. "How was the game, honey?" she would ask with a tone of relief as though an air valve in her stomach had been pulled. She was a nervous, fretting mother who never regained her glow after the death of husband and devoted herself to her son at the expense of her own life. Now both his parents were dead.

Johnny thought back to a few months back when he had come home from work and found his mother in the kitchen. He had finally mustered the courage to ask something he had been thinking about for some time. "What happened before I got home the day Dad died?"

Mary stopped peeling a potato into the sink, a faraway look in her eyes. She turned to her son but did not see him, lost in heartbreaking memory. "I went to check on him, and he appeared to be sleeping so peacefully in bed," Mary said as she took an ambitious drag on her cigarette and blew out a stream of smoke from her nostrils, something Johnny had never see her do. "I knew right away something was wrong." She rested her elbow on the palm of her free hand against her stomach, a long ash dangling precariously from the end of the cigarette. For some reason, Johnny thought of the Statue of Liberty with a weak arm. "I knew he was dead before I . . ." Her voice trailed off, and she regained her focus on her son.

Johnny never thought his mother and father were a great romantic pair, more like partners in the business of family. He provided the income, and she kept a clean house and tended to the boy. Johnny always thought his mother missed the state of being married more than she missed her husband.

As he reached for the phone to make the appropriate calls, Johnny had the strongest sense that Mary O'Brien was in a better place. "Rest in peace, Mom. Rest in peace," he said softly.

*   *   *

Johnny gave the eulogy at Our Lady of Lourdes. He spoke of her dedication as a mother and wife. "She always put family first and herself last," Johnny said as he looked over the packed pews that seemed to meld into one amorphous mass of humanity. "Never did she raise her voice to me. No," Johnny said with a catch in his voice, "Mary O'Brien offered only encouragement and always looked after my best interest."

Johnny had rented the banquet room at the Knights of Columbus for after the funeral. It was on Cedar Lane, at the corner of Old Georgetown Road, no more than a couple blocks from his home. It was a rather plain, spacious space with long tables and folding chairs, but everyone came: his buddies, the neighbors, and folks his mom knew from Our Lady of Lourdes, where she had been a faithful attendee every Sunday. Though nothing fancy—a side of roast beef and sides such as boiled potatoes and coleslaw—it was a splendid affair. Johnny went from table to table, sharing memories about Mary O'Brien. "Some of my happiest times," an old neighborhood woman said, "were when I was having coffee in the morning with your mother before we began our day." She dropped her gaze for a moment and then looked back at Johnny. "It was never quite the same when she began working and could no longer attend."

Later that night, home alone for the first time, Johnny sat at the dining room table, nary a sound in the house. He remembered the morning before his father died, his mother in the kitchen wearing her smock apron with tiny red polka dots, the filter-tipped cigarette between her fingers while in the other hand a spatula stirred a pot of stew on the stove. She had looked over her shoulder and smiled a greeting. "Hello, honey." Never did Johnny remember her more happy.

He got up from the table, went to the drawer in the kitchen, got out his mother's apron, and brought it to his nose, inhaling her scent. He heard her voice whisper in his ear for the last time, "It will be okay, honey. It will be okay."

*   *   *

Johnny inherited the house and money his mother had in a savings account. That was all that remained from her life—a little house on a hill and a few thousand dollars. Johnny wondered if his mother wasn't finally at peace from a life gone askew.

What remained of Johnny's life? It was the 1970s now, and less than ten years before he turned forty. He woke up each day wondering if it was his last. He felt alone, having no family left, with Aunt Bess long dead. He was slowly slipping into a shell, his dating life barely existing, only Friday Night B-ball breaking the routine.

Danny's lease on his apartment was up, and Johnny asked him to move in. Tip followed shortly after. Danny, now a CPA, had taken a position as an auditor with the Department of Commerce. The work, he told Johnny, was uneventful and boring, but it offered security, and once home, he never thought about it. Tip, who had graduated from Maryland with a degree in history, was working for a swimming pool company that Danny's cousin, Tommy Leonard, was a partner in. In the spring, Tip cleaned pools, repaired faulty equipment, and over the course of the year performed any other maintenance work that might need doing. He was the kind of guy who, once he found a job he liked, wasn't going to change. Money meant very little to Tip; peace of mind did. So when all three of them got home from work, they were ready for whatever.

Johnny decided to remodel the basement, and Tip and Danny pitched in. They put up drywall and beadboard paneling, tiled the floor, and hung a ceiling. "Told you that construction job would pay off," Johnny told Danny.

Johnny searched around and bought a dinged and dented round oak table with six matching chairs and then got a deal on a bar and mirror from a tavern up in Frederick, Maryland, that had gone out of business.

"How are you going to get a big old bar moved from Frederick into the basement?" Danny asked.

"I've already measured and planned everything out," Johnny replied. He smiled his rueful smile and said, "Of course, I will need you and the boys for a day."

Johnny rented an eighteen-foot box truck with a back lift and enlisted Tip, Brad, Brian, and Danny to help move the bar. Off they went early one Saturday morning up I-270 to Frederick with Brad and Brian following in Brad's car. When they arrived at the bar, the owner was waiting out front.

Inside, there were boxes and crates littered about the dimly lit space that still had the stale smell of beer and tobacco. Along a back wall were four massive disassembled pieces of the bar. "Oh, man," Danny said at the challenge before them. He tried to lift one of the pieces, and there was no give—these things were heavy.

"Not to worry, Danny boy," Johnny said. "I told you—I've planned it all out." He turned to Brad, Brian, and Tip standing shoulder-to-shoulder, inspecting the work ahead with wary eyes. "We can do this. We will do this."

"Ah, hah." Danny laughed. "Using the down-to-the-last-play pep talk, are we."

Johnny raised his eyebrows and smiled playfully. "Come on boys, we—

The owner interrupted, "Just you five boys?" He was an older man with a seen-it-all demeanor.

Johnny put his hand on Brad's shoulder. "The big boy here counts for two."

The owner scratched the stubble under his chin, eyeing Brad over, who at thirty was still a fit and imposing figure. "That's a big old boy, all right, but I figure you're still short a man. That oak wood is heavy."

"Have faith," Johnny said, "have faith." He motioned to his friends. "We are the boys from Bethesda. The whole is greater than the sum of the parts." He clapped his hands one time, similar to after he'd call a play in the huddle. Johnny thought how Mickey was missing out on something he would die to be part of. Besides Johnny, nobody enjoyed the camaraderie of the boys more than Mickey, but he had a family obligation that he could not get out of.

They lifted the awkward, heavy pieces one at a time onto two carts placed side by side. After they got everything loaded, Johnny paid the man in cash, and off they went.

Back at Johnny's house, they rolled the pieces of the bar to the front door one at a time and then lifted them up, with Brian and Brad, the two strongest, in front carrying the brunt. Tip and Danny managed the back section, and Johnny directed from inside the house through the front doorway—he had taken the door off the hinges—with no more than an inch clearance on either side. Then they lifted each piece back onto a cart and rolled them to the basement door in the kitchen, which Johnny had also removed, and then slid the pieces down the steps.

After they carefully maneuvered the long rectangular mirror, which had been wrapped in canvas, into the basement, the boys helped Johnny reassemble the bar and hang the mirror. He had all the proper tools and knew exactly what to do.

Finally, they were done. But Johnny wasn't done with them yet. "All right, boys, I believe we need to christen this fine establishment." He paused and looked around the space—the mirror hanging on a back wall behind the bar, the shiny beadboard pine-paneled walls, and the fire-engine red tile floor with a herringbone brick pattern. With the round table and chairs in a corner, it looked like a cozy little tavern. "All I need is some fine stools for my fine bar," Johnny said, grinning at the sight before him.

The ring of the telephone broke the moment. "It's Mickey," Johnny said, holding the phone in one arm and resting the receiver between his shoulder and ear. "Wants to know what we're doing. Little Liar's, little seven-card stud?"

"I can play for a couple of hours or so," Brad said looking at Brian, who had ridden over with him.

"Sounds like a plan," Brian said.

Mickey arrived within twenty minutes and took a seat at the table. Johnny had his boys back together again in the old neighborhood. They played for four hours, drinking beer and eating pizzas from the Raw Bar that Johnny had bought half-cooked and then reheated in his oven. There was something about being in that little white house on the rise next to Ayrlawn that added a bit of nostalgia to being in each other's company, so very comfortable with people you trusted like no others—guys you had grown up with, guys whose faults you knew and they yours, guys who accepted you for who you were, united by a bond of loyalty and affection for one another.

When Brad and Brian were about to leave, Johnny said, "Wait. I forgot something." He scooted upstairs and came down with what appeared to be a small, rolled-up carpet. He unraveled it on the card table. It was a tapestry of the dogs playing poker, the one with the St. Bernard chomping on a cigar, keenly looking over the chips at the bulldog while the other dogs looked on—a classic. Everyone broke into great guffaws and laughter.

"That is perfect," Brad howled. "Perfect."

And a perfect day it was for all, especially Johnny.

Over the next month, Johnny bought six oak bar stools at a yard sale in Potomac and then refinished the bar, staining it with a dark patina and finishing it off with a coat of wax—beautiful it was. To finish out his clubhouse, he carved, sanded, and stained a red cedar sign, The Bethesdan, and hung it from anchor chains over the bar. And to top it off, he installed a keg under the bar.

All Johnny needed was an excuse to get the guys over. So he set up Wednesday night at seven as poker night. For a few years, they had a blast, but some of the wives complained. And it was difficult to get up and go to work the next day with only five hours' sleep, so eventually it was only Tip, Johnny, and Danny playing stud poker with a closing time of no later than midnight, though a few times they did break the rule.

By the third year of the three bachelors, Johnny had lost a roommate. Tip fell for a girl who was a lifeguard for his pool company. Shortly after, he was engaged and then married.

"Well, Danny boy, we're the only ones left," Johnny said as they sat at his bar, looking at their reflections in the mirror. They had just returned from Tip's wedding in Annapolis—a great time, but now the reality of it was sinking in.

Danny asked Johnny if he ever thought about finding a girl and getting married. "Never be another Maggie," Johnny said with a shrug.

"Are you saying you'll never get married?"

Johnny reached up and ran his fingers across the letters of the cedar sign he had hung over the bar. "It's like with the Bethesda Colts and at WJ. I'll never meet another group of guys like what we have with the boys." He reached over the bar and placed his mug under the tap for a refill.

Danny slid his empty mug to Johnny. "Don't you want kids?"

Johnny stayed silent while he filled his mug and then Danny's. "Some things," he said, tapping the bar with his knuckles, "some things aren't meant to—" He stopped abruptly and then said, "Hey now, what's with all this serious talk, Danny boy?" He raised his mug to his best friend and said, "And then there were two."

Danny clinked Johnny's glass and said, "Wonder if I will ever meet the right girl?"

A few years later, Danny met a new waitress at the Raw Bar. Tina was the daughter of a doctor no less, and had graduated a few years back from Maryland. She was his first real girlfriend, and after the second date, he told Johnny that he knew she was the one.

One Sunday afternoon, Johnny and Danny were up at the Raw Bar watching the Redskins. The place was packed with folks cheering on the home team. Tina was waiting on the entire back room. She was a rather tall girl with a keen mind and an easygoing personality. She clipped her dark brown hair on both sides of her face with barrettes, revealing a strong yet beautiful countenance with a sweep of cheekbones, a perfect combination of beauty and character. But what really drew Johnny's attention was her smile that transmitted a certain hospitable warmth, an angel's smile.

Tina hustled around the room amongst the din as she took orders and served tray after tray of burgers and pizzas. "Tina, two more pitchers," a guy in a group at the round table hollered out.

"Coming right up, Pete." She went behind the bar, where the bartender was busy, tapped out two pitchers, and darted over to the round table. "Anything else, guys?" she said as though she had all the time in the world.

Johnny and Danny were at a table in the corner near the bar. Johnny had been watching the game with one eye and Tina with the other. As the room erupted in cheers when the Redskins made a big play, Johnny leaned over to Danny and said, "She's a keeper, Danny boy. She's a keeper." He was looking right at Danny but not seeing him as he said, "She's your once-in-a-lifetime girl."

Johnny was Danny's best man and organized the bachelor's party at a bar near the White House that was owned by Jeff Edwards and Brian Tansey, a couple of frat brothers of Danny's from Maryland. The Twenty-First Amendment was a two-story joint with a DJ in a crow's nest on the first floor and a cozy little bar upstairs. It was a wild, raucous place on weekends, with nurses galore from George Washington Hospital, rowdies from Maryland and Northern Virginia, and college kids. At least one fight broke out every weekend, keeping the bouncers on their toes. It was a loud, boisterous, hell-of-a-good-time place.

The bachelor's party was held upstairs, and the boys were all having a grand time. In moments like this, Johnny could put his heart condition completely out of his mind as he watched customers wandering in, awestruck at the sight of his boys downing shots of Wild Turkey, bellowing, braying, laughing uproariously in an all-for-one camaraderie that touched Johnny at the core of his being. These were his boys.

Danny, who was feeling no pain screamed, "What?" when Brad announced that he was heading home for the evening. "No," Danny said incredulously, "you can't leave."

"Watch me," Brad said.

Brad was halfway down the steps when Danny, standing with Johnny at the top of the steps, called him every name in the book for leaving early. Brad turned and flipped him the bird. Johnny tried to guide Danny back inside. Danny started back, and then for who knows why, he tossed his empty beer bottle over his head in the general direction of Brad. Johnny heard a *ploop* and turned back to see Brad clutching the top of his head. Johnny realized what was about to ensue and started leading Danny over to the bar as the stomp of footsteps stormed after them.

Johnny knew Brad was mad, but he also knew he wouldn't hurt Danny, who took a seat next to Tip. Brad came into the doorway and boomed, "McKenzie." His face was beet red, and he reminded Johnny of a mad bull. Brad stormed toward Danny, when one of the outsiders, a little guy, tried to block his path. Harper shoved him across the room as if he were a flea, landing him unceremoniously on a table, pitchers of beers flying every which way. Brad then pushed Danny hard into Tip, knocking them both ass over teakettle off their stools. Before Johnny could intervene, a swarm of the abused guy's friends attacked Brad, who was throwing them off as if they were annoying pests. But the guy he had midget-tossed across the room got a few licks in while his buddies where ripping and shredding Brad's brand-spanking-new shirt off his back.

Johnny knew this situation was one he was helpless to prevent and also rather amusing to observe. Brad was in no danger and looked like the Hulk, snorting through flaring nostrils before he lunged at the little guy, roaring, "Just let me get my hands on you." But this fellow was quick on his feet and bolted for the exit with Brad clomping down the steps after him.

The boys all went outside to watch Brad in hot pursuit down Pennsylvania Avenue, but the little guy was way too fast. Brad stopped to catch his breath, bent over with hands on knees. His antagonist stopped and hooted, "What's the matter, big boy, tired?"

Johnny yelled out at Brad, "Give it all you have, *suuun*. Give it all you have." Tip, Brian, Mickey, and Danny laughed until it hurt as they watched Brad in his tattered shirt running down Pennsylvania—his quarry long gone—screaming and cursing at the buildings.

The next morning, Danny stumbled into the kitchen bleary-eyed and gripping his forehead. "Oh, man," he moaned.

Johnny poured a cup a coffee and handed it to him. "Little under the weather, Danny boy?"

Danny took a grimacing sip of coffee. "I feel bad about what happened to Brad last night."

Johnny handed him the wall phone in the kitchen. "No time like the present."

Danny nodded. "Yeah," he said as he began to dial.

"Hey, Brad, this is Danny. I'm sorry—"

"Are you kidding? That was a great time," Brad howled so loud into the receiver that Johnny could hear him clearly. "I got a knob on my head and a dandy of a shiner under my right eye." Brad laughed his deep, rumbly laugh. "Best time I've had since my last kegger in college when the cops came and broke out the nightsticks."

"You're not mad at me?" Danny said as he made a *can-you-believe-it?* face at Johnny.

"Hell no," Brad replied.

A week later at Danny's wedding, Brad still had a bruise under his eye and a knot on his head, but he wore them both like a badge of honor. That was how the boys rolled.

CHAPTER 12

ALONE AGAIN

Johnny settled into working and living by himself. Working alone was no problem—he had been doing it for years—but coming home year after year to an empty house was dispiriting, sapping his zest for life. Other than Friday Night B-ball and volunteering for bingo at the Knights on Wednesday nights, he was in a rut. Bingo, though, did break the week up for him. He walked about the room, giving out change and kibitzing with the mostly elderly players, many of whom were chain-smoking characters. "Sonny, can you give me a light?" an old fella asked Johnny, who then borrowed a lighter from one of the other volunteers.

"Here you go, sir," Johnny said as he steadied the shaky liver-splotched hand holding the cigarette. His thanks were a sharp, cricket-like *click-click* of the tongue followed by a brief paused and then an exaggerated squinty-eyed wink accompanied by a pronounced nod of the head. Bingo was a hoot.

Johnny realized his life was routine, yet he couldn't muster the gumption to get himself out of it. Or more exactly, he hadn't a clue what he could do differently. He wasn't going to marry and have children, so what other options did he have?

He was mulling this conundrum over in his mind as he pulled into his driveway after a long day of planting shrubs and mulching. Tired as he was, he never minded paperwork and such in his office— his parents' old bedroom, his desk at a window with a view of Ayrlawn.

Johnny paid a couple of bills and then checked his calls. While he crunched out numbers on his calculator for a job estimate, he peered out at Ayrlawn to see if there were any kids playing. More often than not, the place was empty, except during the summer when there were Little League games. Oftentimes, looking down at Ayrlawn, he thought back to when he was young, remembering the smell of the air on a crisp autumn day, the shouts and laughs of boys at play, and the overall sense of being part of something special.

After finishing up in his office, Johnny put on minestrone soup that he had made over the weekend—a two-day affair, not adding the seasoning and spinach until the second day—and then he threw together a salad.

After dinner, he stretched out on the sofa to delve back into a turn-of-the-century novel. The story was about a family on a small farm in Kansas and the struggles they endured to make a go of it. Johnny loved reading books about a simpler time in America, a time when he would have been oblivious to his heart condition and could have lived out his life without a worry until his bad ticker gave out. He would have never known what hit him. He imagined himself back then with Maggie as his wife and Johnny Junior helping him out doing chores around the farm. How grand it would have been, and maybe he could have made it long enough to see his son grow into adulthood. More and more, his imagination was becoming a companion, an old friend with happy-tired scenarios. He snapped back to reality and turned in for the night, to begin it all over the next day, alone again.

Johnny was the only one of the boys who was single; the others were all married with children. The only time he saw his old friends was Friday Night B-ball and an occasional party that he usually attended solo. Some of the wives had arranged dates for Johnny, but he remained his elusive self, never allowing a woman too close. Often now, the woman would break it off, realizing that Johnny was a no-go on marriage. The breakups only added another layer of disappointment. He not only missed the sex but also the company of a woman who made him feel more complete, although he knew he was fooling himself.

At the beginning of a relationship with a woman who was a friend of Danny's wife—an attractive, fun companion—she had the look of finding someone special. "He's so charming, witty, and *so* good-looking," the woman had told Tina.

After the inevitable breakup, she told Tina, "Dating Johnny was like taking a beautiful ride in the country and having the car run out of gas even though the gauge read full."

When Danny relayed the comment to Johnny, his only reply was, "I could not have said it any better." Danny then asked why. "She wasn't Maggie," was the best he could come up with.

Here he was, pushing forty years old and facing the stark reality of his mortality. How much time did he have left? Hopefully more than his sedentary father. Johnny's job provided plenty of exercise, he rarely drank more than a few beers on Friday nights, and his diet was good, especially during gardening season. Johnny had continued his mother's garden in the backyard and grew tomatoes, spinach, carrots, squash, and some other root vegetables. He ate fresh salads from the garden from July through November, and at the end of the season, he canned tomatoes that he used in pasta sauces and soups in the cold months. He was doing his part trying to get through the next decade unscathed.

Johnny hadn't seen a doctor in over twenty years and had considered making an appointment with a cardiologist for a thorough battery of diagnostic tests to see how far along his heart muscles had thickened. But what good would it do? He still wouldn't consider a heart transplant. *It is what it is,* he thought as he was digging a hole to plant a dogwood. It was the beginning of another spring season as a landscaper—Johnny's fifteenth.

When the hole was three times the size of the root ball wrapped in burlap, Johnny gently lowered the tree into the hole. He always enjoyed planting dogwoods, not only for the beauty they brought to the property and neighborhood, but also because he was providing the best opportunity for the tree to live a full life. The dogwood, unlike the oak, had a relatively short life—sixty years at best. It was susceptible to maladies that could shorten its life, and Johnny always made sure to plant them in the shade and provide a mixture of moist soil and compost around the roots. He would then return to water them for the first two weeks. After that, it was out of his hands. He had done all that he could.

Sometimes at work when he allowed his mind to wander, he reexamined his journey in life. He was long past what if. However, he sometimes wondered about Maggie, if she had married. He imagined so, he thought as he slit open a bag of compost and mixed it with soil in a wheelbarrow. And did she have children? She would be a wonderful mother.

"Excuse me."

Johnny turned to see a woman standing a few yards away with her arms folded across her chest, her head cocked slightly to the side, a question in her eyes.

"Hi," Johnny said.

"Do you have time to look at my yard?" She tilted her head over her shoulder in the direction of the house next door. It was a home that had been a neglected rental for years and had recently sold. The realtor who lived in the neighborhood had told Johnny that a widow with two children had bought it.

"Sure," Johnny said through his easy smile. "I'm Johnny O'Brien, by the way." He wiped his hand on the front of his jeans and offered it.

The woman, who appeared to be in her mid-thirties, hesitated for a moment and then shook his hand, her palm soft but her grip firm. "Carol Donaldson," she said. She was a dark-haired beauty with willowy lashes flickering over great green eyes. There was something of the hippie about her, like a perfectly aged flower child.

They went over to the front of the red-brick colonial, the yard in desperate need of upkeep. The lawn was patchy and weedy, ivy grew uncontrollably and dug into the brick mortar of the front façade, and the garden along the picket fence was a jungle.

"My money's a little tight right now," Carol said with a hopeful look in her eye.

"Well—"

Carol interrupted, "You have a little twig in your hair." Johnny searched the top of his head. "No," Carol said as she reached toward Johnny, hesitated for a moment, and then removed the twig planted above his ear. "It was in one of your curls." Her eyes brightened, and they exchanged shy smiles.

"Thank you," Johnny said as he brought his hand to where the twig had been. "I'm always getting something stuck on me." He smiled, and then she smiled, and then as if they both realized they were getting ahead of themselves, their expressions returned to the business at hand. "We'll work something out," Johnny said. They exchanged another look. It was an undeniable look of mutual attraction.

The first time Carol and Johnny met Tina and Danny for dinner at an Italian restaurant across the DC line, Johnny was in rare form. "Did I ever tell you about the time Danny got sideswiped by a character named Crazy Jimmy?"

"No," Tina said, "but I bet it took place during the glory days of high school."

Johnny grinned, his dimples halfway up his cheeks. He turned to Carol and said, "See what I have to deal with?"

"I'm on Tina's side," Carol said, flashing her snow-white teeth that looked like pearls on a string.

"Of course you are, Carol, me dear," Johnny said in an Irish brogue. "Now where was I?" he said, returning to his normal voice without missing a beat. He waved his finger in the air as though just remembering. "Ah yes, Crazy Jimmy . . ."

Soon, Johnny and Carol were an item, seeing each other every weekend. She would hire a babysitter, and they would often go over to Johnny's and have a drink and dinner, enjoying the few hours they had together, just the two of them. After dinner, they would go to his room and make love, her body lean yet downy, clinging to him as though never wanting to let him go. He could feel her pain in their lovemaking, the little flinches when he caressed her velvety skin, the little grunts of pleasure and anguish when he entered her.

Afterward on one occasion, Carol broke into sobbing tears. "What is it, Carol?" Johnny said, though he had an inkling.

"It's Tim, my husband," she said in a choking voice as she sat up in bed, bringing the bedsheet up to her shoulders as though hiding something. "I feel as if I'm betraying him." Johnny put his arm over her shoulder and held her, wiping away a tear from her cheek. She turned and faced Johnny with a look of honest appraisal. "I never enjoyed his company the way I do yours. Never."

Johnny brought the sheet down from her shoulder and kissed her, his tongue finding hers. As their bodies entwined, sending a surge of arousal through him, that little voice whispered, *You're in way over your head.* But there was something about her, the pain of losing a husband with two children that drew him to her as though they were comrades sharing a similar fate. He told himself he would marry her in a second if not for his condition. Or was that an excuse? Was it just that part of him that was content in his loneliness, entrenched in his cycle of routine and having become a creature of habit?

Not only was Johnny letting his guard down with Carol, but her kids—Billy, age nine, and Allie, seven—who like Johnny had lost a father. He understood what those two lovely children were going through, and it drew him to them. When he got off work early on Saturdays, he would come over to Carol's and spend time with Billy and Allie, losing himself in their company, telling stories, playing board games, taking Billy down to Ayrlawn to shoot hoops. He almost began to feel like a part of the family. He tried his best to submerge that queasy feeling in his gut that he was letting this go too far and making it all the worse in the end, but he couldn't help himself.

Johnny invited Carol and the kids to his July Fourth picnic down at Ayrlawn, which he had begun the previous year for his customers and friends. He provided a couple of kegs and burgers and dogs, and people brought grills and side dishes. Mr. Harper and some of the other parents attended—three generations of family—the more the merrier. Mr. Harper was now in his mid-sixties but still had that same commanding big man presence.

"How's my quarterback doing?" he said to Johnny over at the keg.

Johnny handed Mr. Harper a plastic cup of beer and began filling another. "I'm fine, Mr. Harper."

"Call me Bob."

Johnny turned off the spigot and looked up at his old coach. "I can't do that, Mr. Harper. It wouldn't seem right."

Mr. Harper tilted his head off to the side a little, his eyes shining. "You were the best damn quarterback I ever had." He nodded in affirmation and then raised his beer to Johnny, who tipped it with his.

"That was the best time of my life, Mr. Harper, playing for you."

Mr. Harper nodded silently, a nod meant for Johnny alone. Mickey and Danny came up and greeted their old coach, who nodded one last time at his old quarterback before he growled, "Well if it isn't my tight end and halfback."

For the remainder of the day, Johnny schmoozed like a politician fighting for reelection, talking merrily to one and all. Carol's kids had a blast, both of whom now adored this new man in their lives. Johnny tossed a baseball with Billy. "You have a good arm, Billy. I bet someday you could be a big leaguer." The little boy didn't say anything, but the look of pride written across his face spoke loud and clear.

Johnny then took Billy and Allie and some other children down to the basketball court to shoot hoops. "Place the bottom of your left hand under the ball, Allie, and push it with your right toward the basket." Try as she might, Allie's shots fell way short of the basket. So Johnny lifted her up by the waist so that she was nearly touching the rim, and she swished the ball through. "I made a shot, Johnny! I made a shot!"

Johnny spun her around and brought her down face to face, her round, rosy-cheeked face smiling big. "That was great Allie," he said as he whiffed her little girl scent of bubble gum and baby shampoo. *You're in deep—way too deep,* came from the little voice in the far recesses of Johnny's mind.

Later on, Johnny organized a potato sack race, cheering the children on with much enthusiasm. By dusk, the only folks left were Johnny, Carol and her kids, and Danny and Tina and their three-year-old son, Brendan. Johnny invited them back to his place for a nightcap. "One for the road and a game of War for the kids."

The McKenzies were leaving early the next day for Tina's parents' place in Charlottesville. Danny turned to her with a *what do you think?* look. Tina said, "Sure, sounds like fun." Johnny saw in her eyes that she realized how much this day meant to him.

Back at his place, Johnny played cards with the kids at his poker table, and the adults sat at the bar, nursing a glass of wine or a beer as they watched Johnny, animated and giggling along with the kids as he slapped his cards on the table. The children were entranced by him. "Johnny, I won the hand. Johnny, look," Allie shouted.

"Great girl, Allie, great girl." Johnny patted her on the head and smiled his marvelous smile.

Then Allie blurted out, "Johnny, are you grown-up or a kid?"

"Hah." Johnny laughed with delight. "That's the nicest thing anyone has said to me in years."

"John-nee," Allie said with a childish plea, "tell a Scruffy story."

146

Johnny looked over at the bar, a big grin across his face. "A quick Scruffy Lomax tale before we call it an evening?"

"How can we not?" Tina said as she held out her hands as if to welcome him to the stage.

Johnny told of Scruffy and Needle Nose prospecting up in the Kosar Mountains. "It was cold as only Big Bear could be in the springtime," Johnny said, eyeing each one of the kids before continuing. He went on to tell a five-minute story with the two prospectors panning for gold and thinking they had struck it rich; taking a difficult journey back to town and then the assay office, where they discovered it was fool's gold; and ending back at the Lone Wolf Saloon with Scruffy buying a round for the house.

"Pardners," Johnny said in his best sideways Scruffy voice, "I may not be rich in gold, but I have me an abundance of good friends." Johnny looked around the room for a moment and settled his gaze on Allie. "And that, young lady, is all an old prospector ever needs in this life."

Carol was Johnny's first in-deep girlfriend since Maggie all those years ago. Back then, he still considered himself a kid, but now he was a man and Carol a woman with two children to raise. He knew he couldn't let it last, but God help him, he wasn't able to stop himself. Soon Carol had that look of stardust in her eyes, as though she had found the man for the rest of her life. Johnny was having trouble sleeping at night as he wrestled with this impossible situation. He continued to see Carol but with a more even-keel approach, not being so charming or funny. Of course, she sensed this and asked if something was wrong

"Of course not," Johnny said too quickly. "Nothing at all." But soon they had come to a bump in the road, an invisible bump that Johnny had conjured up.

He still spent times with the kids but tried to keep a distance, and Allie picked right up on it. "Johnny, don't you like us as much?" she asked during a game of Hearts with her and Billy.

Johnny had been going through the motions of playing, trying to ratchet down his enthusiasm. He was taken aback by this childish perception and was speechless for a moment, both children looking at him as though they had figured out that something was not right. "Oh, no, Allie pal. I'm just bit tired from work. That's all." But like their mother, the children were on to him.

Johnny wanted to go back to his old ways with these great kids, but it was as though his subconscious was conspiring against him, like a protective shield against that moment in the future when he cut the cord and returned to being Mr. Lonely. He had to, because if he did marry their mother and then died on them, what effect would that have on them—losing two fathers within the span of a few years? He could not do that to them or their mother.

And then the inevitable came when Carol called and asked if she could come over and speak to him. It was a weekday night, so Johnny knew something was up.

They sat in the living room, still decorated with his mother's old furniture: the old plaid sofa in need of upholstery work situated under the bay window, two end tables with lamps, coffee table, and a pair of high-arched chairs that were family heirlooms. Carol sat facing Johnny on the sofa, her heartbreakingly green eyes telling him she sensed what was coming. She told him that she had received a job offer to return to Wisconsin, where she was originally from. "It'd be near my parents, who could help with the kids." She looked down blankly at her hands. "I asked for some time to think about it."

Johnny leaned forward, fingers laced together, forearms on knees. "I think you should take it," he said.

Later that evening, Johnny went out back to ponder things. He stood at the back edge of his property, the sky awash in stars, Ayrlawn slanting in the indiscriminate shadows of moonlight. How much simpler it was as a boy down there, heart condition and all its effects.

But in the here and now, another good woman had left him, or more correctly, he had allowed her to walk away from him. The fact that Carol was already a widow made it easier, he told himself, for she didn't need to go through that experience again. He had allowed himself in deeper with her, enjoying the company of her and her children, and now they were out of his life. He would never forget Carol's expression when he had told her to take the job. There was a wrinkle of hurt mingled with a frown of not understanding, a look that said, *Who are you?* Could he leave her thinking that of him? He needed to tell her the truth.

When Johnny pulled in front of Carol's house, he saw a light on in the living room, the upstairs dark. He imagined Carol had told the kids about moving back to Wisconsin. He could almost hear his name rolling off Allie's tongue. "What about John-nee?" He glanced over the yard that he had transformed from disaster to immaculate: the thick blanket of grass shimmering in the moonlight, the newly planted shrubs lined evenly, everything trimmed and neat.

He tapped on the door and a suspicious voice said, "Who is it?"

"Johnny."

The door opened, and Carol appeared in a green terry cloth robe, a present from Johnny. He ached to wrap his arms around her as they looked at each other, her eyes squinting as though trying to make out what was coming next.

"Can I talk to you for a minute?" Johnny lifted his hand toward the inside of the house.

She stood with arms folded across her chest, her face blankly noncommittal. "Okay," she said and then walked into the living room.

"May we sit?"

Carol sat in one of two matching love seats facing each other with a coffee table in between. The glow from the gas fireplace gave the dimly lighted room a muted, flickering aura. She offered her hand to the other seat.

Johnny leaned forward, hands on knees, and looked at Carol. "I need to tell you why."

Her expression said, *Go on.*

"I have a terminal heart condition and could die anytime now."

Carol brought her hand to her gaping mouth and stared at Johnny.

"I thought you deserved to know."

"Oh my God, Johnny." Carol reached for his hand and laced her fingers through his, her touch warm and inviting.

After a few questions and answers about Johnny's disease, Carol said, "I'll stay here and be with you for as long as you have."

"Carol," Johnny said as he placed his other hand over hers, "think about the kids. They don't need to lose another father. I don't want the kids to see me . . ."

"Oh, Johnny," Carol said through a great sigh. "Yes, the kids."

"Go to Wisconsin," Johnny said with a catch in his throat, "and make a new life for yourself and them."

"I will always love you, Johnny. Always."

*   *   *

Once again, Johnny was alone, running his one-man business from a new Ford van he had purchased after years with the old banged-up bread truck. Actually, he did all right for himself. All of his business was within a six-mile radius of his house. Life was too short to spend much time traveling from job to job. And he was funny about who he worked for. He had done a few jobs in Chevy Chase Village, an upscale, older neighborhood packed with old and new money, and then stopped. It wasn't worth the aggravation of dealing with all the nitpicking.

He rarely left Bethesda for a job. He rarely left Bethesda, period. But he took four days off every July, working extra hours beforehand to go off to Bethany Beach where Brian, Mickey, and Danny took their families every year. It had been become a tradition, Johnny staying at the Breakers Hotel right on the boardwalk and meeting the others at the beach every day, showing up with a beach chair and towel. The wives would have lunches packed, and Johnny would rent three umbrellas—he always insisted on paying. "My treat," he would say.

When he wasn't taking the kids into the ocean, "Uncle Johnny" was tossing a Frisbee or helping them make sandcastles with moats. Every year, Johnny bought a bushel of crabs, and they would all sit around in the backyard of Danny's rental drinking beer and cracking shells, Johnny recalling a toned-down version of some escapade from the past, the boys laughing uproariously and the wives shaking their heads—"Oh, you boys."

This year's annual trip to Bethany had been no different, allowing Johnny a few days to take his mind off things. On his last night at the beach and after crabs at Danny's place, everyone had called it a night except for Johnny and Danny. They sat across from each other at a table covered in crab-stained newspaper, a wicker basket of empty shells and claws nearby, and the scent of a warm summer evening and Old Bay lingering in the air.

Johnny had been in fine form, cracking everyone up with a story about Irish Shammy O'Toole and the leprechauns. It was a kid's story, but he had everyone entranced. Oh, how he could weave a tale, that melodious voice of his effortlessly shifting from one character to the next. When he had finished, the kids wanted another, and Johnny told a yarn about Scruffy Lomax that included every one of the kids in the story and had them helping with the narrative. It was just as enjoyable for the parents.

"Scruffy is a little old gnarly fella who grew up in Big Bear, Alaska, a long time ago. He had a little mangy dog with red fur." Johnny stopped and looked at Brian's son, who was about ten. "What should we name the dog, Brian?"

The boy looked at Johnny. "Hmm," he said, "something like Red." Young Brian hesitated and then said, "But that's not it."

"How about Rusty?" Johnny replied.

The boy's eyes widened with the wonder of it all. "Yeah, Rusty," he shouted.

And so it had gone that evening.

But now, as Johnny and Danny sat in the humid night air with barely a hint of a sea breeze, Johnny had the look of a depleted actor: the eyes narrow with an edge of tiredness, the passionate mouth, so alive and animated earlier, now a twisted wrinkle. "Grand time, this evening, grand time," he said.

"The kids loved your stories, Johnny," said Danny. "We all loved them."

"You know . . ." Johnny paused for a moment, looking up into the night sky at the moon spilling light and casting shadows. He looked back at Danny. "Some folks have great and happy lives the entire journey."

"It's your heart, Johnny," Danny said, "isn't it?" They stared at each other through the chasm of time, two childhood best friends facing the truth.

Danny raised his hand as if he had overstepped a boundary line, a line that Johnny had tacitly and figuratively drawn in the sand all those years ago at Hot Shoppes when Danny learned of the heart murmur. "I'm here if you ever need me, Johnny."

Johnny nodded his head once, a faint smile hovering in the corner of his mouth. "I lost a father at age ten, and still I had a great childhood."

"Talk to me, Johnny."

"Oh, Danny boy, you are a good friend," Johnny said, standing up. "Thanks for a great time."

He shook Danny's hand and walked away into the shadows, the faint roar of the ocean riding in on a suddenly arriving sea breeze and escorting him into the night.

Johnny suffered another loss when downtown Bethesda went under a redevelopment phase, and with it, McDonald's Raw Bar closed its doors. Johnny bought the ship's wheel clock in the back room and hung it in his bar at home. All that Johnny had left was Friday Night B-ball. He never missed a Friday, always the first one there, sweeping the floor beforehand with a long-handled dust broom. One of the school janitors, Nat Jefferson, was a good basketball player and was always there. And on any holiday that landed on a Friday, Nat would open the gym with each guy contributing five bucks.

The '80s were the glory day days of Friday Night B-ball, with as many as seventeen guys showing up to play. So they spilt up into three teams and played winners for two hours, running up and down the court, competing for all they had. Johnny had been a guard on the team at WJ. He was a fine passer and always got everyone involved in the game. Besides the guys from WJ, there were others who showed—friends of friends and a brother-in-law or two, and Craig Wrenzel and Joe Morrison, former jocks from BCC, WJ's archrival. Both had been a year behind the boys. When they first came out on the court, there was a wariness on both sides, old rivalries still present, especially Craig, who was a Vietnam Marine combat vet and crackled with aggression on the basketball court. But soon Craig and Joe melded into the group as all realized how similar they were, and that basketball and beers afterward were the only place and time where they could revert back to their youth.

The boys now drank their beer in the parking lot outside the school gym that had residences within shouting distance and downtown Bethesda looming nearby. The tail end of rush hour traffic at the intersection of Old Georgetown Road and Arlington Boulevard was white noise in the background. But none of it stopped the boys from hooting and hollering and kibitzing about the just-played games, sports, or women. They were a collection of aging relics who didn't want to let go of something they had their past—competition and camaraderie.

One Friday night after b-ball, the boys broke up into clusters in the parking lot, conversing and arguing in a good-spirited way. "Lagos," Danny said in a raised voice from one group over to another. "You couldn't guard your grandmother."

"Mac," Brian retorted, "at least I can make a layup."

"What?" Danny screamed.

After a while, the decibel level increased, and it reminded Johnny of Tara Road back in the day, and in a way it was the same thing. They were no longer kids, but they were carrying on much as they had in high school.

And then Johnny had another flashback when three squad cars of Montgomery County's finest pulled into the parking lot. Three police officers walked toward the boys with humorous looks of disbelief.

"We got a call about teenage boys drinking," the sergeant in charge said. "I wasn't expecting a group of men in their forties."

"Teddy Dolan, me lad, Erin go bragh," Johnny said in his finest Irish brogue. "'In service to one. In service to all.' How are things at the Knights?"

"I should've known who would be the ringleader of such a gathering." Sergeant Dolan shook his head as he took in the group of middle-aged men in sweatpants and T-shirts, some still wearing blue basketball jerseys with "Friday Night All-Stars" scrolled across the front. A small but congenial smile nestled in the corner of the policeman's mouth. "Just keep it down to a roar, Johnny, and we'll be on our way."

And so it went. The officers packed up and left and Johnny always kept it down to a roar.

Chapter 13

Holding On

Year by year, the numbers at Friday Night Basketball dwindled, from injuries to knees and shoulders to busy lives with work and children. The remaining players would get a call every Friday afternoon at work from Johnny, making sure they were going to play. Everyone received the same call. "Five on the nose. Don't be late. I got a cooler of ice-cold beer for after in the parking lot." Mingled with Johnny's spirited voice was a trace of desperation. "You'll make it then, Danny boy? Now, don't let me down."

Danny would always respond, "Johnny, have I ever let you down?" The core group remained, other than Tip, who had bought a home up north in Frederick County and was rarely seen anymore other than at Johnny's Fourth of July picnic.

Five-on-five was a thing of the past, so they played full-court four-on-four. That involved a lot of running. But most of them, especially Johnny, were still in good condition. They couldn't jump as high or run as fast, but they could still play a hard, competitive game. And even at this advanced age, they were still arguing and bickering during the course of a game with Johnny, the voice of reason, settling things down when Brad would bark, "Doyle, you been calling the same cheap-ass foul for over twenty years." That same look of utter disbelief would come over Mickey's face as he gave Brad an earful. Johnny always felt a twinge of pride at his boys being boys.

Socially, the boys rarely got together, since they had new groups of friends with parents of children's classmates and neighbors. This left Johnny out. He began dating single women or divorcees, women anywhere from ten to nearly twenty years younger than him. Over the years, he had sometimes brought a woman to his picnic at Ayrlawn but never the following year. He either didn't have a date or there was a new one in her place. The consistent thing about it was that none of them had children. Johnny had decided that he didn't want the extra heartache when the inevitable breakup came.

When Tina and Danny met Johnny and a date at a restaurant in Bethesda for dinner, he couldn't hide the edge of sadness about himself. He had recently turned fifty—eight years more than his father so far—and his date was in her mid-thirties. Johnny looked young for his age, much as he had always looked, his handsome face unlined and his hair full and still black save for flecks of gray on the sides.

Johnny knew they were nearing the end of this relationship that he had started off with enthusiasm on the first few dates, listening intently as she told of her recent divorce and cheating husband. But after a time, Johnny, like it or not, began comparing her to Maggie, who wouldn't have pouted when he didn't want to go to the opera or spent way too long putting on makeup. Mostly she just wasn't Maggie.

Johnny saw the concern in Danny's eyes. His good friend, who never lectured Johnny or questioned why he had chosen such a life for himself, only sat there and tried to pick up the conversation. Johnny's date was polite and attentive, but there wasn't a sparkle in her eyes or an uplift in her voice. Everything about her said, *We're at the end of the road, and it's time for me to get off the Johnny merry-go-round.*

After that breakup, Johnny promised himself to go cold turkey, swearing off women, not wanting to put himself or them through the rollercoaster ride that was *The Courtship of Johnny O'Brien.* But then the loneliness and the ache in his loins for a woman's body would get the best of him, especially that winter, when the days were short and the house seemed engulfed in a veil of gloom and doom. It was one of the worst periods of his life. There had been a cold snap with heavy snow, and Johnny was stuck in his house. His van was no good driving in such conditions, swerving and sliding every which way. He went around the neighborhood helping neighbors dig out from under. It was great coming in for hot chocolate or soup and reminiscing about old times. "I remember watching you play for the Bethesda Colts," one older, long-time resident said. "I told my wife you were Johnny Be Quick."

But then when things turned slushy and icy and the yards were covered in a blanket of crusty snow, Johnny was stuck at home, reading and cooking by himself. Each night, he went to bed early, and each night, sleep was difficult as he played the what-if game. What if he had married Maggie? By now, their first-born would have been in college. Or if he had married Carol, her kids would be nearly grown, and they all would have had some wonderful years in each other's company. He would lay there in bed, eyes wide open and alert, hands clasped behind his neck, saying to himself, *What if?*

By the following spring, he had returned to long work days, digging and planting and meeting clients and giving out estimates. The entire process reinvigorated Johnny not only mentally but physically, and the promise to swear off women now seemed like an impossible thing to do. There were no two ways about it—he needed the body and the company of a woman. He wondered if he were not addicted to the entire process of living like some reptilian creature that could eat one meal that would last for months before having to go out and hunt again. That's what he did—hunt for women through the smokescreen of his ever-present good looks and lighthearted charm, though he now began to wonder if they were a curse.

On a Sunday morning in May under a brilliant blue sky, Johnny went to the farmer's market in downtown Bethesda under the guise of looking for fresh vegetables. He spotted her in line to buy tomatoes and struck up a conversation in his easy, likable way. "The question of the day is beefeaters or heirlooms?" he said as general conversation. She turned to face Johnny, an expression of sharp appraisal on her face. It was a pretty face with delicate features, thin yet sensual lips, a flush of pink in her dimpled cheeks, and wide-set hazel eyes that bespoke of a difficult patch in her life. It was her eyes that drew him. They looked sad, as though she needed to be held tight and told everything would be all right. She turned out to be in her late thirties, recently had settled an acrimonious divorce, and had no kids. He had been there and done that, but he was in once again.

They dated for six months, and then it was over. Afterward, Johnny told Danny, "I'm the in-between guy who provides comfort until they're ready to find Mr. Right." He lowered his head and shook it. "I'd be a liar if I didn't say they provided me comfort, too."

"You could be their Mr. Right," Danny said. They looked at each other in silent recognition of Johnny's unhappiness. They were in the parking lot after Friday Night B-ball, only Johnny and Danny left—two men in their fifties—on a cool November night under a sky clustered with stars, the inviting aroma of Chinese food wafting in the air from North China Restaurant a block away. They were two survivors on an island shrinking from the inexorable tide of time.

Johnny reached into his cooler and removed two freezing bottles of Coors. He twisted off the caps and handed Danny one. "I own a house free and clear and a business, and I come and go as I please. It could be worse, Danny boy. It could be worse."

"I don't get it, Johnny," Danny said, staring into his beer. "You're my best friend, and I feel you've been holding a secret from me for years." And then he squinted hard at his friend, his lips one tight line.

It was a look Johnny had never seen from Danny. "You let Maggie go all those years ago. Why? Why, Johnny? And Carol? What the hell?" There was a tone of controlled rage in Danny's voice, a pent-up tone that was years in the making. "You were Mr. Right for both those good women." Danny flung his hand out. "Shit, you could've had any woman you wanted."

Johnny sighed so heavily that it seemed to break something loose inside him. "Let me fill you in on why I won't ever be Mr. Right. I'm living on borrowed time, Danny."

"Your heart?" Danny's voice had a sudden tremor to it.

"It's a condition I inherited from my father, and if that isn't bad enough, I can pass it on to my progeny."

"Jesus, Johnny. Jesus." Danny stood leaning against the hood of his car with a look of utter disbelief, as though all the blood had been drained from his face. "What about surgery?"

"My only hope would be a heart transplant," Johnny replied, "but that's high risk. I could be dead in a month if my body rejected the new heart." He took a swallow of beer and wiped his mouth with the back of his hand. "And my gut tells me it would reject it." Johnny shrugged and said, "And the irony of it is that I don't feel bad. Matter of fact, I feel good. So why risk a new heart that my body may reject?"

"How much time have you got, Johnny?"

"Like I said, Danny, I'm on borrowed time." Johnny looked at his old friend, who looked for all the world as if it were his life that had been given the death sentence. "I know you have sensed something was wrong ever since that incident at Shoppes all those years ago when you overheard I had a heart murmur."

"Yeah, I did, but I didn't think it was . . ." Danny's voice trailed off.

"Danny," Johnny said with a rallying rise in his voice, "come on. I'm not dead yet." Johnny laughed and lifted his chin toward Danny. "Now, come on, I say. Enjoy this fine evening with me."

Danny forced a smile and nodded. "You're right."

Johnny looked off over across Old Georgetown Road and pointed to a one-story white building with a glass front, surrounded by bigger, newer, sleeker structures. It had changed hands many times since Bethesda Billiards was a tenant. "Remember when Spike Ridley stole Tip's bike from Ayrlawn and I got it back when he parked it outside the pool hall?"

"Yes, I remember," Danny said, still trying to absorb Johnny's shocking news.

Johnny took a swig of beer and raised it to Danny's. They clinked bottles, and Johnny said, "You're a good friend, Danny." He nodded as if to confirm his words and said, "I know you'll keep this between us."

"I won't tell anyone, not even Tina."

Johnny cleared his throat, and the last remnants of seriousness left his face. "Now, will you give me a smile, a real Danny boy smile, and let us enjoy the little time left on this grand Friday evening?" He took another drink of beer and smiled his charmer.

"Yes, you may," Danny said, smiling too hard but still trying to please his dear friend. "Remember the time you saved Mickey's ass at Brown's?"

CHAPTER 14

A NEW GIRL

It was a Sunday in late April, the air pleasantly brisk and breezy. In the last few years, Johnny, who had recently turned sixty, had gotten into riding a bike on the weekend on the many trails in the area. During the week, he tried to work as long as he could before going home to his empty house. Mondays were the worst, and Thursdays were bearable because Friday Night Basketball was coming soon. He didn't mind working alone, his mind and body absorbed in the task at hand. He had not tired of his job, enjoying talking with his clients beforehand and the general sense of well-being from the great outdoors. But after eating dinner, everything, as it had for years now, slowed down into a mind-numbing state of ennui. He had trouble concentrating when watching TV, and even reading was becoming a chore. Sometimes he even drove to the Tasty Diner in Bethesda, ordered a coffee, and sat in a booth reading to be in the company of people. So on Sundays, to escape his house, Johnny would take a bike ride. His bike was nothing special, a ten-speed hybrid that he could ride on or off trail.

He rode through his neighborhood, crossing over a few major roads into other neighborhoods, meandering his way into bustling downtown Bethesda and onto a paved trail that used to be a B&O Railroad line that ended in Georgetown. The trail was crowded for the first couple of miles, and Johnny was careful not to run into joggers or other bikers.

Eventually the traffic tapered off, and he was riding along the C&O Canal on a wide stone-dust trail. This was where Johnny would lose himself in the thick green foliage, the bright, fresh smell of spring in the air, and the chirps and warbles of birds darting about in the trees. The trail ended under a massive highway ramp, and he had to ride up a steep hill, and Johnny was in the heart of Georgetown with its eclectic, upscale shops in brick row houses built long ago. He locked his bike on a parking sign and decided to stroll around, ducking in and out of the ultra-expensive stores: $2,000 for a trench coat, $3,500 for an eighteenth-century desk.

Johnny wandered up a side street and came upon a sign for an art exhibit in front of an upscale row house with a brick wall in front, ornamental wrought iron pickets, and wide marble steps leading to the front door, which was wide open. Johnny figured, why not? Past the cavernous foyer and through an archway was a long and wide room with artists standing on both sides, their pictures hung behind them as they talked with admirers, a table between them.

One artist, a woman with long, sandy-colored hair that fell behind her shoulders, was standing alone. Her artwork had large, simple strokes of a variety of colors in loosely brushed squares and triangles, each one seemingly so simple yet so serene and peaceful. She was tall and lean with a long but well-formed face highlighted by a sweep of cheekbones and a high forehead that suggested intellect. But what drew Johnny were her eyes, large and gray with a slant toward the temples, which gave her face an enchanting aura. Johnny smiled at the woman. "Hi."

She studied Johnny for a moment, her eyes taking him in as though he were a subject to be painted. "You don't remember me, do you?" she said with a trace of a rasp in her voice, an interesting voice.

Johnny looked at her closely, and she returned his gaze with a bold, unblinking but not unfriendly look.

"Yes, you were a class behind me at WJ." Johnny raised his hand as he searched his memory. "You were friends with Danny McKenzie's sister." He drew back and smiled as though he had won a prize.

"You're Johnny O'Brien," she said through a shy yet confident smile. "You were big man on campus my junior year."

"That was a long time ago."

"I never thought you even knew I existed."

"Your name was Jean."

"Still is," she said with a laugh. "Jean Plover."

Johnny turned his attention to her art. "Let me guess—some type of abstract expressionism."

"Very good."

And very good it was. They reminisced for a good ten minutes before Jean had some interested customers. Johnny hung around, watching Jean talk about her art.

"Landscape and space are my inspiration for my art," she told one couple. "I look beyond the here and now in my creations." While she talked to potential customers, she glanced over every so often and caught Johnny's eye, then returned to her business at hand. There was a mutual look of attraction, a look from Jean that said, *Stick around.*

There was depth to this girl, this woman, Jean Plover. When she would get a break, Johnny would slide over and ask her about herself. He learned she had studied abroad in Paris and now lived in Philadelphia, where she had been making a living selling her art for over twenty-five years. She didn't talk like anyone he had ever known. "Americans live to work," she said softly to Johnny during a lull. "I live through my art." And when she was finished, Johnny helped her pack her paintings in the trunk of her big Audi sedan. They then went to a coffeehouse, where Johnny learned she lived and painted in a loft in a converted warehouse.

"You live a different type of life," Johnny said.

She replied, "So I'm told."

Johnny asked if she came down often to DC. "If there were something or someone that interested me, I would. I definitely would." Her words were spoken with assurance, but in her eyes, there was something girlishly shy. He reached for her hand, and she took his, her touch warm and inviting. Johnny hesitated for a moment and then said, "Will you come next weekend and stay at my place? I will cook for you."

Jean squeezed his hand and put her other hand on top. "Yes, I would like that. Indeed I would."

*   *   *

Johnny woke and sat up on the edge of his bed—his parents' old bed, actually, that he had moved into his room after his mother passed—and rubbed the sleep from his eyes. He had slept well except during a booming, thunderous storm in the middle of the night, after which he quickly returned to sleep. He stretched his arms over his head, smiling to himself at what the day might bring him. Jean was coming later in the afternoon. She would be the first girl from WJ since his senior year. It struck him that his life was coming full circle.

After dressing, Johnny went into the kitchen. He was going to make spaghetti and meatballs, a recipe of Maggie's that he had been fine-tuning for years. Also on the menu was Italian garlic bread and spinach salad with cherry tomatoes and red onions. Normally after he cooked the meatballs in a skillet, he added them to the sauce. But today he would hold back in case she was a vegetarian. He didn't know why he thought that, more a gut feeling, and if she wasn't, he could add them later.

Johnny looked out the kitchen window to see if there was any damage from the storm. There were some small limbs and branches scattered in the yard, no big deal. A whooshing gust of wind swayed the treetops, and then a cracking sound, like a rifle shot, drew his attention to a tree in a neighbor's yard. A large branch with splayed limbs was dangling precariously from a power line that wobbled from its weight. Then the branch fell, crashing onto the side of the street. The power lines were okay, but that was a close one, Johnny thought as he took a paring knife to a red pepper.

After the sauce had been prepared, including canned tomatoes from the garden in back, he slit the crusty bread down the middle; slathered one side with olive oil, parmesan cheese, and herbs; wrapped it aluminum foil; and put it in the fridge. He then made the salad and set the table. And there it was—everything good to go other than boiling the pasta.

Johnny stepped outside. The sky had cleared some, billowy clouds cruising across the grayish-white sky. There was a lingering dampness in the air, the temperature brisk but with enough promise for Johnny to consider a bike ride before Jean's arrival. He liked the feeling after a hard ride; his legs would be achy, but he always felt a sense of reinvigoration. He decided to ride the bike trail down to Georgetown and back without any stops—one long burst of sustained energy, get home for another shower, then a shave, and then wait for this intriguing woman, this artist, whom he had not seen or thought of in over forty years before their chance meeting.

*   *   *

Johnny cruised down Oakmont Avenue, the bike ride nearly complete. He had that happy-tired feeling he used to get as a boy. Now he was coming home to spend the evening with a woman he barely knew, but one he found himself comfortable with in her presence. He was also curious as to what she was all about. He had no idea how this evening would turn out. Would she sleep in his bed or want private quarters? He would let it all unfurl naturally, looking forward to spending time with Jean, getting to know her over a drink or two and see where it took them.

Johnny gripped the brake handles as he turned right on Hempstead and coasted around the corner. Jean's Audi was parked in the driveway behind his van. As he rode up, she emerged from the driver's seat wearing a knitted green sweater that fit her body like a glove and calf-length corduroys revealing a swell of shapely calves, her long hair in a ponytail. She looked stunning.

"Hi there," Johnny said. "I hope you haven't been waiting long." He got off his bike.

"Five minutes," Jean said easily. She then opened the back door and removed a hiking knapsack.

"I'll get that," Johnny said as he took the bag from her. "I see you travel light."

"I'm a simple girl."

They exchanged smiles and then Johnny said, "I made spaghetti and meatballs, but I thought you might be a vegetarian."

"Me?" she said in an amused tone. "I'm a carnivore."

"Ah," Johnny said as he offered his hand toward the front door. "You fooled me."

"You wouldn't be the first."

Her matter-of-fact tone caught Johnny off guard for a moment before he motioned toward the door and said, "After you."

Johnny placed Jean's bag on the foyer floor and asked if he could get her anything.

"I'm fine. You go clean up and"—she shrugged—"we'll go from there."

After a quick shower and shave, Johnny found Jean sitting at the bar, pouring herself a glass of Chablis. "I was wondering where you were," he said as he went behind the bar and poured himself a draft.

"I like this room," Jean said, looking around as she checked over the oak table nestled in the corner and the checkered floor. She stopped at a picture of the Bethesda Colts on the wall. She went over for a closer look, and Johnny followed. "There you are," she said, pointing to Johnny kneeling in the middle of the front row, flashing his brilliant smile. "You had charisma even then." She was peering closely, her artist's eye seemingly missing nothing. "You look happy there."

"I'm happy you're here," Johnny said.

Jean looked at him, her eyes reading his face, and he felt a seductive tug of desire drawing him to her haunted beauty. She leaned in to him, her body tight and firm, her hands sliding up his back to his shoulder blades, her fingers kneading his muscles. It was at that very moment that Johnny knew where she would be sleeping tonight.

* * *

Maintenance work on the school gym put Friday Night Basketball on hold for the summer, and Johnny hadn't seen any of the boys for a while.

While trimming a hedge row in the neighborhood, Johnny spotted a familiar SUV pull up. Danny got out and waved. "Hey, Johnny," he said with cheer, "aren't you getting a little long in the tooth for this?"

"What brings you to the old neighborhood, stranger?"

"Just stopped by to see my mother." Danny looked around at the large paper bags filled with yard waste and gardening tools nearby.

After Johnny asked about Danny's mother, he wiped beads of perspiration off his forehead with a bandana and put it in the back pocket of his shorts. He motioned Danny over to a shade tree and sat under it on a stack of bags of mulch. "Do you remember a girl a year behind us at WJ named Jean Plover?"

"Of course," Danny said, peering down at him. "She was a good friend of my sister, free-spirited and good-looking. She answered to the beat of a different drum."

Johnny nodded as he reached behind himself and picked up a plastic bottle of water off the ground. "I met her at an art exhibit."

"When did you get interested in art?"

"I'm not—or I wasn't, but I took a bike ride down to Georgetown and decided to wander around a bit. She's an abstract expressionist and was displaying her art." Johnny took a swallow of his water and offered it to Danny.

"No thanks," Danny said to the water. "How long has this been going on?"

"Couple of months."

"Why didn't you say anything about her?"

"I'm telling you now." Johnny stood and took another swallow of water. "She lives in Philadelphia and comes down when she can get away from her studio." He swept bits of mulch off the front of his shirt and looked at Danny as if he had something more to say.

"Yeah?" Danny said. "What else?"

Johnny grinned self-consciously. "I've even taken the train up to Philly a couple of times." He grinned again and said, "She's inspired me to start painting."

"Are you shitting me?" Danny said as he pointed to Johnny's water and took a swig. "Have you told her," he said, lifting his chin in the direction of Johnny's chest, "about your heart condition?"

"Soon," Johnny said with meaning. "Soon." He scuffed the ground with his boot and looked up at his good friend. "It's funny. I've made it this far, and some guys from our class at WJ have already raised a family and died. And I'm still here." He shook his head, stared at the ground, and then looked up. "Could've, would've, should've." They looked at each other for a moment before Johnny said with a lift in his voice, "Anyway, Jean told me she had a couple of guys who wanted to marry her, but she broke it off. Her art comes first."

"What's she like?"

"Different," Johnny said. "I'm not sure I have her figured out." He lifted his shoulders and threw his hands out to the side. "Women have been saying that about me for years." He laughed. "Now it's my turn."

"So," Danny said, "what's a typical date for you two like?"

"Why don't you and Tina come by my place this Saturday for a barbeque and see for yourself?"

*   *   *

Johnny was in the backyard icing down a cooler with beer, white wine, and bottled water when Danny and Tina appeared around the side of the house. Johnny greeted them with a handshake for Danny and peck on the cheek for Tina.

"So where's this new love in your life?" Danny said.

"Danny," Tina said in a mild scold.

Johnny looked over toward the sliding glass door. "Voila," he said as Jean, dressed in a dark T-shirt, jeans, and flip-flops, emerged holding a platter of egg rolls. "Danny, Tina, I'd like you to meet Jean Plover."

"Hello," Jean said in a cheery voice as she placed the tray down on a picnic table. She glanced at Danny and said, "Well, if it isn't the big brother. How's Sissy?"

"Good," Danny said. "You look exactly the same."

Jean flashed a gorgeous smile at Danny. "You and your buddies," she said, tilting her head toward Johnny, "were the big jocks in school. You guys seemed to live in your own little orbit." Her tone was that of one observing some strange species.

"Some of us still do," Danny replied, shooting a glance at Johnny, who grinned back.

Johnny took drink orders and asked everyone to have a seat at the table. By the time Johnny returned, Tina and Jean were talking about an art exhibit going on in DC, and Johnny mentioned Monet and his influence on the art world.

"Monet?" Danny said as he dipped an egg roll into duck sauce. "Jean, what have you done to Johnny?"

"She's opened new horizons for me, Danny boy," Johnny said as he glanced over at Jean, her eyes smiling sunshine. But behind the veneer were strength, independence, and nothing needy about this new woman in his life. After a round of drinks, Johnny took Danny over to the grill, where he cooked burgers, he and Danny with beers in hand while the girls had wine at the picnic table.

"So what are you painting, Johnny?" Danny asked.

"I'll show you after we eat," Johnny said. "I think you'll be surprised."

"Will I, now?" Danny looked over at Jean, so perfectly at ease chatting with Tina. "She might be a keeper."

Johnny flipped a burger, sending flames shooting up from juices leaking onto the hot coals. He turned over the rest of the burgers, put the lid on the grill, and closed the air vents. He glanced at Jean, who looked over and smiled at Johnny. "It feels right being with her, Danny boy," Johnny said.

After eating, Johnny looked across the picnic table at Jean and Tina. "Can you girls excuse Danny and me for a moment?"

"Sure," Tina said, looking at Jean for a hint.

"It's Johnny's secret," Jean said.

"Come on, Danny," Johnny said, standing.

"Man," Danny said, "you're full of surprises."

Inside Johnny's bar in a corner was an easel covered by a drop cloth. Johnny removed the cover to reveal a painting of Ayrlawn. The sky was crystal blue, the field with patches of grass and dirt, the hill near the big backstop with the trees in their proper place, and the silo with Moo Moo in all her faded-green glory. Over near the basketball court, two boys were playing catch, one with dark hair and the other, a lefty, with light brown.

"It is so good," Danny said, drawing out *goood.* "I can almost hear the echoes from the past." He leaned closer. In the left corner was a signature in sepia ink—*Johnny O'Brien*—and in the right corner the title, *The Beginning.*

"I want you to have it, Danny."

"I can't take this." Danny turned to Johnny. "I know how much all of this means to you," he said, returning his gaze to the painting.

"You must," Johnny said as he put his hand on Danny's shoulder. "You will appreciate it when . . ." His voice trailed off, and in the silence, something passed between the two best friends.

"I am honored," Danny said with a catch in his throat. "I truly am."

* * *

That September, the gym opened back up, and they were down to six guys playing with Johnny still calling to make sure they were coming: Johnny, Danny, Brian, Mickey, and two janitors. The games were now half-court with little running, still a good workout, but there weren't nearly as many foul calls and little arguing. Afterward the boys would frequent a bar in Bethesda filled with young adults the same age as when they first started going to the Raw Bar.

Bethesda had changed a lot over the years, becoming a progressive, upscale destination with trendy restaurants for folks with money to spend. There were still some bars Johnny and friends found suitable, and they still enjoyed drinking a few beers in each other's company but in a more low-key manner. One new addition was Steve Newman, Mickey's old adversary, who had become a wealthy stockbroker and philanthropist—Steve "Dude" Newman, the desperado. Mickey and Steve had long since buried the hatchet and were good friends. The remaining boys were like a dying breed who gathered together on Friday nights to swap lies about the old days. Johnny wasn't the last man in the bar anymore. "Jean is driving in tonight from Philly," he would say. "Gotta run, boys."

Johnny felt different, as if trying to adjust to something he hadn't experienced since Maggie Meyers—a woman who was on equal footing with him. He realized that he had been spoiled by how easily women had always fallen for him over the years. The relationships, other than Maggie, were one-sided, with Johnny holding all the cards and always looking for a way out of the game. He had never left the gathering after b-ball to meet up with a woman until Jean.

He had been procrastinating about telling Jean about his heart, but tonight he was considering it. He said good night to the boys, but not before Mickey said, "Johnny, we got to meet the woman who gets you to leave early."

"In due time, Mickey, in due time."

When Johnny arrived home, he found Jean's car parked in front. *Right on time*, he thought. And it was also time to let her know about his condition. He hadn't felt this comfortable with a girl since Maggie. If she didn't want to continue dating, he would understand, but he needed to let her know what the situation was. And if she said yes, how good would that be?

As he approached the front door, it opened. Jean stood there tight-lipped, her eyes devoid of emotion. "We need to talk, Johnny. I wanted to tell you in person."

*   *   *

After Jean left, Johnny went downstairs to the bar and punched a number on his cell phone. "Hey, it's Johnny," he said tonelessly. "Can you come over? . . . I'll tell you when you get here . . . . Thanks."

Johnny sat in the darkness, waiting. He turned at a tapping on the sliding glass door. A figure stood outside, and Johnny went over and unlocked the door.

"What's going on, Johnny?" Danny said as he entered and turned on the light switch.

"Thanks for coming, Danny." Johnny motioned him over to the bar, and they sat next to each other. "Jean," Johnny said in a raspy whisper.

"What happened to Jean?"

"She's done with me." Johnny reached for a mug of beer on the bar that had been barely touched.

"What's going on?"

"Jean arrived, and I was going to tell her about my"—Johnny tilted his head toward Danny and whispered—"condition. But before I could, she told me that it was over between us. A first for me, Danny boy. She's been seeing an artist in Philly." Johnny took a meager sip of his beer. "I had even met the guy," Johnny said, staring at his hands folded on the table. He looked up at Danny. "And here's the kicker. He's a good twenty years younger than me." Johnny sat back in his chair, scanning the room before his eyes settled on Danny. "She fooled me, Danny boy. She fooled me." He gave his head a little shake and said through a sigh, "Or maybe I fooled myself."

"You really liked her," Danny said, more as a statement of fact.

"Yes, I did," he said softly. "Just when you think your life's heading one way—a good way—it takes a detour." Johnny winced and looked off. "I enjoyed her company. No pressure. We'd sit in the backyard," Johnny said, raising his chin toward the sliding glass, "or sit at the bar—she loved the bar—and talk." Johnny looked at Danny. "Not only art, but how we interpreted this life—ambitions, goals, all the BS."

"You'll meet someone else," Danny said.

Johnny squinted in doubt.

"You going to be okay, Johnny?"

Johnny took a sip of beer and then another longer one. "Aren't I always?"

"You gonna show next Friday at b-ball?"

He offered Danny a smile of reassurance, his Johnny smile that had charmed everyone he had ever come across. "Of course I will, Danny boy. It's all I have left."

Chapter 15

Slipping Away

Johnny returned to the gym the next Friday. He had called Danny beforehand. "You're coming to b-ball, right, Danny boy?" There was a false bravado in his tone, a plea of desperation.

"Have I ever let you down, Johnny?" Danny replied with his pat answer.

"No," Johnny said solemnly, "you never have."

They played three-on-three, with Johnny giving it every ounce of energy he had, as though he were trying to sweat out the effects of Jean's dumping him for a younger guy.

Afterward, it was just Johnny and Danny at the Rock Bottom Brewery, sitting on stools at a small round table in the bar area. They were by far the oldest two in the place, though there were some forty-year-olds mingled amongst the twenty-somethings. They ordered a couple of pale ales, and then Danny asked Johnny how he was doing.

"Better than when you saw me last week." Johnny leaned forward and said, "Thanks for coming by."

They paused as the waitress came over with their ales. "Anything else, gentlemen?" She smiled big as she stole an admiring glance at Johnny.

Johnny smiled his Johnny smile. "We're good, thanks," he said kindly. She held his gaze for a moment and then smiled back before darting away.

"You still got it, Johnny."

Johnny shrugged nonchalantly. "I could nearly be her grandfather." He then took a thirsty swallow of his ale and let out an "Ahh . . . that's good stuff."

They small-talked sports and a few reminiscences from the past. It was needed time spent with his best friend, but on the drive home, Johnny felt as if he had been going through the motions, the exuberant personality and hilarious stories a thing of the past. He was a toned-down—way down—version of his old self, still attentive when listening, a *bon mot* at just the right time, but he felt his passion diminished.

Johnny had outlived his father by eighteen years. He never had expected to make it that far, and for that he was thankful. He would try not to think about how much time he had left and instead concentrate on lifting his spirits. He decided to do what had worked when Maggie departed his life all those years ago: he would *work* his way through it.

He had plenty of jobs lined up to facilitate his plan. And so that Saturday, he worked until dusk and went home bone-tired. He continued at this pace up until Friday, when he arrived at a residence to plant shrubs. It would be a full-day job, but he promised himself he would quit early, rest up before b-ball, and finish the rest tomorrow. There was no hurry, since the family was out of town and wouldn't be back until Monday.

The house was on a hill overlooking Wyngate Elementary School, a place filled with old memories. Johnny couldn't work too hard on Fridays anymore; it was affecting his stamina on the court. The long workweek had eased the pain of Jean's sudden departure from his life and had left him looking forward to b-ball and a few beers afterwards—the simple things in life, Johnny thought as he began to dig. He had over thirty shrubs to plant and a dogwood to install at the front corner of the house. His plan for that day was to dig holes along the neighbor's border in the backyard and then plant boxwoods to allow privacy, then dig the holes for azaleas in front of the house and plant them. He would finish off the day planting the dogwood.

It was late September with a trace of humidity in the air, but the light was distinctly autumnal. It was approaching Johnny's favorite time of the year, which always reminded him of practice at Ayrlawn with the Bethesda Colts. He lost himself in the job at hand, digging and cutting out ornery roots with a hatchet or axe, placing the boxwoods in their holes, and adding the soil and compost. When he had finished planting all five, he took a moment to appreciate his work, the scent of the green foliage lingering in the air.

After finishing the azaleas, Johnny decided to break for lunch. He retrieved his brown bag lunch from the van and sat on the ground under an old red oak, its roots shooting out into the yard, heaving up part of the walkway. The owner, an elderly gentleman in his early eighties, had told Johnny that he would live with the destruction. "It's such a majestic old tree. I don't have the heart to kill it."

And Johnny had agreed. "I admire it," he had said, rubbing his hand over its coarse bark. "The oak is a long-living, tough breed."

Johnny lifted his leg, swept away an acorn under his thigh, and nestled his back against the old oak. The humidity from earlier in the morning had been swept away by a cool breeze. He looked up at flat-topped clouds floating across the blue sky, the sun dodging in and out from behind them. He had lived in this neighborhood for over fifty years now, in the same little white house the entire time. He remembered the first day he had moved in and had discovered Ayrlawn spread out before him. What a sight it was: the basketball court, the long expanse of grass, the big backstop with the hill next to it sprouting a stand of trees that had grown substantially over the years. That first day, his mother had been directing the movers where to put everything, stealing a glance at Johnny from time to time with a look that said, *Isn't this grand?* His father was trying not to get in the way, standing at the doorway and then shuffling into the living room, never staying anywhere too long.

Johnny tried to recall his father's face, and it was like a poor reception on an old TV. It crossed his mind that he had hardly known his dad. Oh, what a shame. Maybe if he had lived, they would have grown close. Johnny shook his head at the improbability of such a thought.

He finished his sandwich and stood. He suddenly felt so tired, as though he hadn't slept for days. "Come on, Johnny," he said aloud, "plant this dogwood and be done for the day."

He dug the hole at the corner of the house and was relieved that he didn't run into any roots, but it seemed to take forever. His body seemed to be winding down, as though ready to go into sleep mode. *Get it planted and get home for some rest*, he thought as he eased the tree into the hole. He took a moment to rest, his gaze settling on the young tree, its branches so frail and spindly with a smattering red berries emerging. The dogwood was an understory tree, living in the shadows of bigger trees, its berries containing a single seed that someday would scatter in the wind to proliferate and hopefully renew life.

Johnny bent down to cut off the burlap when he felt his chest tighten. In all his years, he had never felt such a sensation. He tried to dismiss it as nothing, but when his jaw began to tighten to the point he had trouble opening his mouth, he reached for his cell phone in his pocket. A sharp surge of pain in his chest brought him to his knees. He tried to move his arm to get the phone, but nothing was working as the pain ratcheted up, pounding his chest.

Johnny lay on his side, his life flashing before him: Ayrlawn and his boys, Bethesda Colts, junior high, WJ, Shoppes, the parties, Friday Night Basketball, the Raw Bar and Maggie—oh yes, Maggie.

He tried to say her name, but it was too late. Gasping for air, he closed his eyes and saw Ayrlawn back in the day with the sun dipping below the western sky over the stand of trees on the hill. Echoing in his head were the hoots and hollers of rambunctious boys at play mingled with the sound of a basketball clanging off the metal rim at the asphalt court, the cracking pop of a baseball pounding into a leather mitt. It was autumn, the smell of leaves burning in the street wafting down onto the field during football practice with the Bethesda Colts, the boys' growing bodies straining to outdo each other and working as a team as they did it. "Son, I say *suuun*, give it all you have!" The camaraderie, the laughs, the fights amongst the boys and against whomever—all of it gone with the setting sun.

In his last moment on this earth, Johnny O'Brien saw himself as a boy, his eyes shining, his endearing smile spread across his handsome young face. And for the last time, he heard his youthful laugh that had never grown old.

Go gently into the night, Johnny, me boy, go gently . . .

Made in the USA
Middletown, DE
31 August 2021